RHYONNA'S FRIGHT

A Faery's Challenge to Save Her Realm

Acknowledgements

To my family and friends for all their encouragement.

To SCBWI, Society of Children's
Book Writers and Illustrators, for conferences, retreats,
workshops, meetings, and critique groups
to help writers and illustrators.

To CWC, California Writers Clubs,
for their workshops and meetings to help writers.
To the EAST BAY Critique Group,
started in 1984, and the many people who participated in
and helped with critiques.

A special thanks to the 2012 East Bay Critique group:
Kathy Urban, Kate Tasker, Sarah Wilson, Joanna Kraus,
Bill O'Connell, and Mary Boyce.

To Schelly Gartner for edits and comments about flying.
To Jo Ellis for her developmental edits.
To Sarah Knopp for her suggestions and edits.
Especially, to Carla King for her excellent
Indie BootCamp for self-publishing.

Dedications

To Brauley, Tara, Erin, Sarah, Kate, Lindsey, Alicia, and Tasha when we camped at Liz Lake in 1981, while dragonflies flew, we talked of faeries, and Rhyonna's story grew.

To the novel writing class with Marcy Alancraig at the Senior Center in Albany in 1984 with Amy, Beverly, Cordel, Denise, and Marcy, who helped shape Rhyonna into a twenty-five-page prose poem.

To Sarah Wilson, author and friend, who encouraged farther writings about Faery Rhyonna.

To Janet Murrell for all our days in the gardens weeding, planting, watering, and meeting the garden spirits and the others.

To Mimi Luebbermann where Faeries dance in her gardens and fields at WindRush Farm.

Especially, to Sarah Knopp, my niece and assistant, who sparked the e-publications to start the journey of *Rhyonna's Fright*.

And inspiration from my granddaughter, Julia Kinkead.

paperback - ISBN-13: 978-1-942070-00-9, ISBN-10: 1942070004
e-book - ISBN-13: 978-1-942070-02-3, ISBN-10: 1-942070-02-0
Kindle - ISBN-13: 987-1-942070-10-6, ISBN-10: 1-942070-01-2
audio book - 13: 987-942070-30-0

Library of Congress Number: 2015920651

As Is Productions for BobbieTales
Publisher's Note: This is a work of fiction, a product of the author's imagination. Any resemblance to actual people, alive or dead, or to events or locales, is coincidental.

Book design © 2013, BookDesignTemplates.com
Printed by CreateSpace, An Amazon.com Company
Available on Kindle and other epub devices from e-book stores

Rhyonna's Fright

Story and Illustrations
Bobbie Kinkead

AS IS Productions for BobbieTales
Oakland, CA

Prologue

Happiness for Brawny Rhyonna Faery,
Flying Teacher for the Wee Flyers, is challenged.
During the hot nights of this long summer,
Grayed Creatures steal syrup
from BlackBerry Village.
These thieves drop spores,
which grow into gray fluff
that eats everything sweet.
To save her realm, Faery Rhyonna
must battle Zzuf, this horrid parasite,
who infests her and the others.

TABLE OF CONTENTS

1 - FLYING   1

2 - MEADOW FRIENDS   7

3 - TAWNYEE FLYERS   16

4 - THE TRAP   26

5 - LADYBUGS   30

6 - CAVES   35

7 - THE MESSAGE   41

8 - THE DARE   47

9 - ESCAPE   51

10 - QUEEN FLOREE   57

11 - MAJESTIC   64

12 - HOME   69

13 - SPIDER ERWINA   77

14 - FRIENDS RETURN   94

15 - FAERY FUN   104

16 - FAERY POND   113

17 - FLOWERS   125

18 - OOPS, OFF AGAIN!   135

19 - THE PLAN   145

20 - THE DESCENT   159

21 - THE BATTLE   172

22 - RHYONNA'S FLIGHT   181

23 - GIFTS   189

CONNECTING . . .   198

CAST OF CHARACTERS

Brawny Rhyonna, Flying Teacher for the Wee Flyers

Aide Erstwood, messenger to Queen Floree

Beti Kacie, a Tawnyee Flyer and the First Keeper of the Butterfly Eggs, Caterpillars, and Chrysalis

Caddee, Teacher of the Wee Ones

Dandelion, Rhyonna's flower

Darren Gale, a Tawnyee Flyer, and the First Keeper of the Orb Spiders and Their Webs

Evan Roy, a Tawnyee Flyer and the First Keeper of the Hummingbirds and the Secret of Their Nests

Father Adair, Rhyonna's father

Fish of the Pond

Guard Prior of the Ant Colony

Grayed Creatures, the fluffed Ladybugs

Healer Leanna

Hue the Hummingbird

Keegan, Captain of the Junior Patrol

King Grady of BlackBerry Village

Ladybugs, Protectors of the BlackBerry bushes, eaters of the aphids

Lender, Lizard of the Rock

Majestic, Dragonfly for Rhyonna

Mizzee Bee

Mizzee Queen

Mother Emma, Rhyonna's mother

Myrna, Seamstress and Weaver for the village

Old Gruff the Toad

Old Oakee, Sheegahshee in the old Oak Tree

Prince Blaire, son of Queen Tanya and King Grady

Princess Lessie Shelly, a Tawnyee Flyer and the
    First Keeper of the Dragonfly Grubs

Queen Floree of the Ant Colony by the Lake

Queen Tanya of BlackBerry Village

Rufus, one of four Butterflies

Scout Bryn of the Ant Colony

Scout Fay of the Ant Colony

Scout Neddy of the Ant Colony

Scout Rue of the Ant Colony

Slime the slug

Spider Erwina, the Orb Weaver

Sweet the Moth

Tawnyee Flyers or the four Flyers

Varda, Seamstress and Weaver for village

Zzuf the Parasite, horrid fluff, the mold

Rhyonna's Meadow of Flowers

Rhyonna's Dandelion

is in the Meadow of Flowers.

Rhyonna's favorite rock

is in the center of the Meadow.

In the north are the Oak trees.

In the west Fish Creek passes to a pond.

In the east Berry Creek passes through

the BlackBerry bushes of Faery Village,

by the thistle hill of the Ant Colony,

by the clay caves of Zzuf,

into the Lake.

1 - FLYING

RHYONNA STANDS ON DANDELION, stretches her hands high into the warmth of the day, opens her wings, and sings, "Hello, vast sky!" Rhyonna jumps. "I love to fly!"

Her hands and wings pull down then up using the air to flutter higher and higher. "I'm as light as the air and free as the wind." Then Rhyonna pushes her mighty wings wide open to hover like the birds in the air beside her. "Hello, singing Birds! I'm happiest when I fly."

Looking down at the lake surrounded by the Oak trees, Rhyonna muses on their beauty. "Good morning, trees! You are tiny!"

Rhyonna folds her wings gently to her sides to glide with the wind, singing, "I'm the Flying Teacher for the Wee Flyers in BlackBerry Village."

Fluttering above the Meadow of Flowers, Rhyonna opens her wings to balance in the drifts of currents. Her wings shine luminous yellow-green, almost transparent in the sunshine.

Below Rhyonna flies a hornet, an angry hornet, buzzing, almost a holler, and falls into the flowers, strange. Rhyonna floats down to the meadow and quietly fitters through the flowers just close enough to the hornet. Rhyonna watches the hornet battle gray fuzz on its wings. Her guess is the hornet flew into a spider's web. Rhyonna quietly flitters from the noise; this creature is not one of her favorites.

A gold-green Dragonfly whizzes around here and there, then staring directly at Rhyonna is the Dragonfly.

"Hello, Majestic! What a day."

Majestic pauses his wings, pops, and floats in the air, answering, *"Incredibly quiet day."*

"Majestic, did you see and hear the hornet?"

"No hornet in my territory."

"Then have you seen Keegan? I was to meet him here in the daisies."

"Keegan is near. Rhyonna, best flyer, want to race?"

"Yes, a race to the pond."

The races with her Dragonfly make Rhyonna the best flyer in her village. Majestic, does not fly in a straight line, only zigzags up and down or pivots around. Rhyonna faces the giant Dragonfly, not knowing in which direction to fly.

"READY!"

"GO!"

Majestic flies under Rhyonna, then he dashes to up into the sky. Around into a somersault, Rhyonna pivots, clasping her hands above her head. Rhyonna pulls her wings into a lift. Her second pull catches Majestic.

Of course, the giant Dragonfly pops straight up into the sky. Rhyonna pulls in her wings and pivots into another somersault, pushing her wings out. Then, with all her strength, Rhyonna pulls against the air. After several pushes and pulls, Rhyonna flies beside Majestic. Of course, he pops and turns left.

Rhyonna pivots left, pulling her arms to her sides, fluttering her wings fast. Majestic turns to face Rhyonna, then dives down, down, disappearing deep into the haze around the pond.

Rhyonna takes a huge breath, tucking her wings at her sides, and then dives down into the enchanting haze to Majestic. His metallic gold-green colors reflect light. The giant Dragonfly perches on a willow branch over the water, quietly waiting. Rhyonna stops her dive by pivoting upward, opening her wings, and pushes against the air to stop.

"You caught me, best of flyers."

"Majestic, you waited for me to find you."

"Yes! Must tend my places."

Majestic spreads his wings, pops, and disappears with a deep whiz into a haze of light.

Rhyonna breathes deeply to relax while observing the silver water rippling around the willow roots. Fish splashes in front of Rhyonna.

"See Friend!"

"Fish, you have such good eyes."

"Rest like bug?"

"I'm thinking."

"Think Keegan?"

"Keegan is to meet me in the daisies. While I wait, I'm planning the flying lessons for the Tawnyee Flyers."

"Fly what?"

"A pivot, where one stops in mid-air, turns in the direction wanted, and then pushes with wings forward into a turn."

"Swim now?"

"Sure. My teaching is later."

Rhyonna stands on the limb, tucks her wings tightly, and then jumps feet first into the pond. When her head is above the water, Rhyonna pushes her wings out for balance and moves her arms back and forth to float. Fish slides underneath Rhyonna, who settles on his back, holds tight to his top fin, and takes a long, deep breath. Rhyonna needs one full breath for the ride. A minute for Rhyonna is an hour in Fish time.

Under the water, they dive. Fish's fins swish back and forth to strum a consoling, "Shh, shh." His powerful tail glides with the rhythms of currents. His movements are like the push and pull of Rhyonna's wings. Such strength Fish has.

He follows a stream of water that trills through the openings between roots. The harmonies in the water refresh Rhyonna. Fish weaves through the soft emerald mosses, which intertwine among the earth-scented roots. Rocks sparkle like jewels in the rippling light, which flows around Rhyonna to create a magical watery enchantment.

All too soon, her breath is needed. Rhyonna tugs on Fish's top fin. Immediately, he swims up and breaks the surface of the water. Rhyonna gasps, then breathes. Fish swims her to a sandy beach.

"Fish, you are graceful and powerful."

"Wade, shallow."

"I'll bring the Tawnyee Flyers to you about befriending a minnow, so they have a fish friend."

"Show minnows."

Rhyonna floats off Fish and wades through the clear water onto the warm sand. A rush of warmth blows strong against her like the mellow flow of moss in the water.

With each step on the dirt, Rhyonna struggles to hold herself upright. In water and air, Rhyonna is light; walking on the ground is clumsy and heavy.

2 - MEADOW FRIENDS

STEPPING CAREFULLY through the tall, straight grasses Rhyonna zigzags through the Meadow of Flowers to her favorite rock. Always one flower or another blooms here.

Captivated by sugary fragrances, Rhyonna sits on the dirt. The ground is warm, only a bit too hard. Standing up, Rhyonna picks flower pollen. Spicy white daisy, yellow zestful poppy, and sweet red clover are crunchy pleasures.

In front of her, on the ground is a mound of fluff. Walking closer, Rhyonna shutters, the angry hornet motionless and entangled with gray fuzz. Rhyonna screams and runs through the flowers only slowed by her wet wings.

After a long while, Rhyonna stands by her favorite rock, safe. Large and rough, the rock surges above the flowers. With her wings tucked, her hands find a crack, and her arms pull while her feet push. Rhyonna climbs the jagged surface. Pulling up with her hands is slow finally Rhyonna reaches the top. Her weight is heavy like this rock, not quick and agile as Lender the Lizard, who flees from her.

"Oh Lender, Rhyonna here, wanting your rock to dry my wings in the sun."

Lender cautiously pokes his head from a crack and reaches his tongue forward to smell Rhyonna. Then slowly, grasping the rock with his four legs, the Lizard crawls up the rough surface. He is so slow he resembles a dried stick. His eyes and ears move, observing. Rhyonna admires Lender's steadiness and awareness. Her awareness is just as keen.

"Lender, today in the daisies, I am to meet Keegan. We are to climb into the giant dandelion. He is late. So I'm waiting with you."

Lender the Lizard crawls to Rhyonna and lies down to relax in the sun. Just as Lender, Rhyonna loves the heat and stretches open her wings.

"Lender, did you hear the hornet?"

With silence Lender listens then closes his eyes and continues to sing.

"Lender, you live in the moment."

Rhyonna joins Lender's singing. Making up songs is her favorite pastime, especially singing to the rhythms of the flowers swaying back and forth with the wind.

A blurred buzzing appears in the sweet clover. Cautiously pondering the sound, Rhyonna is relieved to see a bee.

"Hello, Mizzee Bee."

"Buzzzzee, buzzee, buzeee."

Mizzee is most disciplined and attends to exactly what Mizzee needs. Rhyonna is never that busy.

"How is the nectar?"

"Grreeeaat, grreeeatteessstt!"

Mizzee's wings beat so fast they look invisible. Flying is not important to Mizzee, just gathering pollen from flowers, even in the rain.

"And the clover pollen?"

"Theeee BEESSSTT, beeesssttt!"

When Mizzee stops to gather pollen, she is just as diligent, busily walking, reaching, and collecting.

"Have you seen Keegan in the daisies?"

"Izzzzz withee Prinzzzzee."

"With the Prince. He forgot our fun! What can be so important?"

"Fffuzzzzz duzzzzt."

"Dust? That is strange."

Before Rhyonna can ask what kind of dust, with a twist Mizzee is in front of Rhyonna.

"BUZZZZ, BUZZZZ, BUZZZ! zLzzikz zzmzy ZZZonggg?"

"Yes, your song inspires and fills the air."

Mizzee flies to the next flower, busily balancing and gathering. She has superb balance, even with pollen stuck to her legs. Rhyonna has superb balance like Mizzee. For the Tawnyee Flyers' lesson today, they will do balancing exercises.

Enjoying a nibble of the sweet clover pollen, Rhyonna sees four butterflies fluttering among the flowers in the drifts of wind. Their black and yellow stripes almost resemble the dried grass, only more elaborate, special, and yes, lavish.

The butterflies flutter up and then down in a slow, musical wave. One travels over to Rhyonna. He pulls his wings slightly together, floats for a second, and lands feet first next to Rhyonna.

Butterfly Rufus spreads his wings and settles on the rock.

"Hello, Rufus."

Lender the Lizard slides quickly into his crack.

"Absorbing, my dear Faery!"

Slightly moving his wings back and forth, taking up space, Butterfly Rufus ambles around the rock.

"Thinking, tasting, seeing?"

"Only wondering. Have you seen Keegan? He was to meet me and is late."

"Flying in the Oaks, dear Faery."

"So Keegan comes here?"

"Flying with Prince."

"What could be so important?"

Rufus pulls his large wings together.

"Engaging sadness."

"The day is rather dull without Keegan."

Lender the Lizard slowly crawls beside them to sun and continues his silent singing.

"Rufus, your flying is poetic. You float and glide while the air currents move you this way and that."

"Harmonizing perfectly, dear Faery. Pulling wings up. Drifting down slowly in the puff."

"Rufus, do you use gravity?"

"Opening, pushing the tugging. Raising up."

"Your landing is art."

"Gliding landing, art?"

"You hold your wings together and gracefully land on your feet."

"Holding, tasting, dear Faery!"

"Rufus, will you show your skills to the four Tawnyee Flyers?"

"Savoring! Delighting Flyers!"

"And the four Flyers need a caterpillar."

"Finding eggs. Befriending, as with me."

"Yes, Rufus, the four Flyers can protect the caterpillars as they change into butterflies."

"Growing into flight, enjoying!"

Butterfly Rufus stretches his wings up and wiggles his feelers to test the breeze.

"Relishing! Valuing Faeries!"

With a quick down of wings, he is off the rock.

Rhyonna watches three Butterflies flutter with Rufus from flower to flower. The four play together gliding up, then down, and then around like laughter. To fly is play and at the same time power. Rhyonna has power and knows how to play.

"Where is Keegan?"

While searching the flowers to see if Keegan flies to meet her, Rhyonna gasps, "ANTS! Horrid ants carrying the dreadful sap-sucking aphids."

A line of ants moves by the rock. One ant behind another, each carries an aphid up a daisy stem and places the sap-sucker beneath a flower, Keegan's flower.

These sap-suckers drink the BlackBerry's sweet sap, stunting the flower's growth. Then the ants milk the sweet sap from the aphids and in a line carry the sap back to their colony.

Rhyonna wants to crush them. Ants are vile creatures, stealers of life. The villagers hate them.

So strange how they pat each other's heads with their feelers. They never talk, laugh, or sing, only stay on the ground, walking. They never sleep. Wind blows, rain falls, and on and on they walk, although they do drink water from leaves. They have no fun, never feeling or seeing, only stealing food day and night. Ants are tedious.

Once Rhyonna followed them as they carried seeds to their hole. The ants gave the seeds to ants inside the ground. A large ant with fierce jaws raised her front legs at Rhyonna. The ant was Prior, who guarded the opening to the colony. Prior was curious about the Faeries who flew among the flowers. That hill is not a place to visit.

Rhyonna has privileges, flying anywhere at anytime and eating pollen whenever. Faeries are never stuck on the ground to work. Rhyonna has her special time to teach flying lessons.

Looking carefully at the flowers, not one Ladybug eats a sap-sucking aphid. Ants controlling the aphids crawl all over the flowers. Rhyonna carefully inspects each flower. Not one Ladybug. Every flower covered with sap-sucking aphids drinking sweet life. Not one Ladybug anywhere, unbelievable.

Rhyonna loves their fancy orange-red jackets with black spots that cover their tiny transparent wings. The jolly flyers flip here and there looking for the awful sap-suckers. Ladybugs are clumsy fliers and jerk in the wind. Still they fly that long distance into a forest. Rhyonna, the best flyer in the village, can fly over the land to also see the beauty.

A breeze dances with the flowers, Rhyonna asks whoever might hear, "Are the Ladybugs flying to their mating place? This is a bit early in the summer."

The flowers bobble silently in the breeze, puzzled. "The Ladybugs, the Protectors of the BlackBerry bushes, can't be gone." The others in the Meadow stop their song, wondering, and then go back to their day.

Rhyonna nibbles pollen from the sweet clover and wonders why Keegan is so late. Four tiny figures fly close to the bushes. Shadows sprinkled with light filter the shapes. The figures glow. Giggles fall into the breeze.

"My Tawnyee Flyers!"

3 - TAWNYEE FLYERS

OH, NO! The Tawnyee Flyers are alone. This is not good. Princess Lessie Shelly is to be in the village with the Queen Mother and King Father. This is trouble! Teacher Caddee would never allow flying through the open Meadow.

Rhyonna stands, spreads her wings, and quickly pushes off the rock. They know better, or will know better.

At Dandelion, voices sing, "Surprise!" Their giggles fall on the empty flowers. Rhyonna swoops from the sky towards them.

"YOU NEVER . . . "

The giggles turn into frantic screams.

"What are you doing in the woods ALONE?"

The screaming stops; the startled faces turn into begging faces. Four Faeries flutter in front of Rhyonna.

"We need to fly to the lake," begs Darren Gale.

"Darren Gale, as the leader, you are much too overconfident. Flying all the way from the village in not allowed."

The Tawnyee Flyers flitter around, their faces still begging, "Please!"

"We must fly!" demands Darren Gale.

"Please, take us flying, Rhyonna?" asks Beti Kacie.

"Even you, the best flyer, flying here is not the best way to use your gift. Beti Kacie, you always follow Darren Gale. Tell him no. You need confidence."

Rhyonna motions them to Dandelion's flowers.

"What's so important? Why all the hurry?"

"We want to follow the gray dust," says Evan Roy.

"You, Evan Roy, are too quick to say yes to any adventure, then get into situations you cannot handle. Like this one."

"Please, we must follow," begs Princess Lessie Shelly.

"Coming into the Meadow isn't wise. Lessie Shelly, you're much too innocent."

"But, we need to cross the Meadow to follow the Junior Patrol," demands Darren Gale.

"Stop flying around! Settle! Speak one at a time." The four Flyers settle on flowers. "Quiet voices! Go slow! About the Junior Patrol?"

"Queen Mother directed the Junior Patrol to follow the trail of the thieves," explains Beti Kacie.

"Keegan is Captain of the Junior Patrol," says Evan Roy.

"My brother Blaire is Second in Command," brags Princess Lessie Shelly.

"BlackBerry syrup stolen," asserts Evan Roy, who is too excited to sit.

"Stolen?"

"Sticky gray smelly dust left on the berries," says Darren Gale, who is now flying around.

"The acorns turned over," adds Beti Kacie, "syrup spilled everywhere."

"No syrup for this winter," complains Evan Roy.

"Were the thieves ants?"

"No one knows. Captain Keegan and the Patrol follow the gray dust," says Beti Kacie.

Darren Gale heads for the trees.

"Darren Gale, come back here! Where did you leave Teacher Caddee?"

"She is in the village," answers Beti Kacie, flying to a flower and quietly sitting.

Guilty, the other Flyers land on flowers.

Irritated, Rhyonna asks, "Do you know where?"

"Somewhere?" answers Evan Roy.

"Somewhere?" Rhyonna glares at the four.

"Cleaning up the dust," adds Princess Lessie Shelly.

"Then we fly to Teacher Caddee. She looks for you and so do your parents.

"Stand up!

"Get ready!

"One, open wings!

"Two, pull up arms!

"Steady . . .

"Three push down!

"JUMP!

"FLY!"

Four Flyers are in the air flying; Rhyonna flies next to them. Rhyonna is happy with her teaching and maybe a bit too angry. They are spirited, bold, and courageous like her, and excellent flyers. They are ready to fly in the Meadow. Their intensions were good; they did come to get her before dashing off on their own.

Long before the four Flyers reach the village, Rhyonna smells mildew floating through the Oak trees. The four Flyers slow, almost stopping.

"Rhyonna, I'm tired," complains Princess Lessie Shelly.

"The village is just through these Oak trees."

"Can we rest?" grumbles Darren Gale.

The mildew odor grows thick, and the four Flyers fly even slower. Evan Roy flutters to a branch under an Oak and sits. Beti Kacie, Darren Gale, and Princess Lessie Shelly sit with him. Rhyonna settles besides them.

"You four are afraid. The gray dust can't be that bad!"

"The smell makes me sick," whines Princess Lessie Shelly.

Rhyonna expects the four are worried about the discipline they will get when they return. Rhyonna playfully brushes them off the branch into the air.

Slowly, ever so slow, the four Flyers enter the village.

Gray dust floating in the air chokes breathing. Panic looms everywhere. Rhyonna huddles the Flyers together, keeping them beyond the fears of the village.

Acorn pots are overturned; the berry syrup spilled everywhere. Gray tangles run along the sticky ground like on the hornet in the meadow. Rhyonna watches her parents with the help of the villagers stack the empty acorns.

Mother Emma approaches. "Rhyonna, hold this primrose petal to your face, the dust makes one dizzy. These are for the Flyers."

"Is the dust that bad?"

"We don't know what it is," Mother Emma says.

The four Flyers scatter. Rhyonna gathers them and hands each a primrose petal for a mask. They fly to the school.

Teacher Caddee is in the BlackBerry bushes by the schoolhouse. With rigorous force, she wipes leaves. A thick cloud of gloom stirs the air.

Rhyonna pulls the four Flyers back. They settle on the school steps, choking with the uproar.

"Teacher Caddee, I bring these Flyers back to you. They flew to Dandelion."

Caddee stops and looks at them. She stares, blank, dazed.

"Oh dear, I thought they were with their parents." Caddee stands motionless in front of the four Flyers. Then frowning, she asks, "Why did you go into the Meadow?" Caddee cries, "What if something happened to you?"

Looking at the ground, the four fidget and try to hide.

"Caddee, what is that irritating smell?"

"Garlic and primrose in oil," Caddee sobs. "I can never clean all the leaves!"

"What happened?" asks Rhyonna.

"Thieves took the berry syrup and left this mess," whines Caddee.

Slopped on the ground are sweet berries mixed with the fluff, which seems to be growing and stretching. The Flyers flutter around and over piles of sticky broken branches.

Rhyonna directs, "Sit quietly on the school steps. The fluff isn't safe."

Caddee signs, "Gray dust sticks on every bush, ruining the flowers and berries. The BlackBerry leaves wilt with this blight. What are we to eat during the winter rains?"

"Who are the thieves?"

"Grayed Creatures."

"I saw an angry hornet in the flowers with the same fluff. I thought the fuzz was spider webs, then later the hornet was a stilled mound with this same dusty fluff growing on it."

The four Flyers hear and fidget on the steps.

"Did anyone see Grayed Creatures?"

"Keegan and Prince Blaire were up early looking for the Ladybugs when they saw the Creatures carrying off our syrup. Keegan was made Captain of a Junior Patrol because the Village Patrol is cleaning."

"Who flies with him?"

"All his friends and Prince Blaire."

"I know Captain Keegan and Prince Blaire are proud. I would be. Caddee, I want to find out what the Junior Patrol knows. Will you watch these Flyers?"

The four Flyers jump from the steps, fluttering around.

"We want to go," pleads Darren Gale.

"Take us," begs Evan Roy.

"P L E A S E!" chorus the Flyers.

"The fluff is not safe," warns Rhyonna.

The Flyers hang on Rhyonna's arms with insistent faces. Rhyonna gently releases their tightened fingers from her arms and point to the school's steps.

"The Queen Mother and King Father will take away the flying lessons. Then no Wee One learns to fly."

Caddee looks at the Flyers, "They will stay with me." Then she directs, "Here are oils to rub on your arms and face. Wear these webbed masks. Here are brooms. You will sweep the fluff off leaves."

"I want to fly with Rhyonna!" demands Darren Gale.

Rhyonna gives him her stern look. "Help Teacher Caddee! You will have your flying lesson when I return."

Darren Gale sulks in a huffy way with his arms crossed and sits on the school steps. Rhyonna gives him her sternest look. "Stay!"

"I'm off to find Captain Keegan."

Rhyonna hugs her dearest friend Caddee, a long deep embrace. "I'll be back!"

The four Flyers whine. Rhyonna shows her angriest look. "Help, Teacher Caddee!"

Grumbling, they pick up the brooms, dipping them into the smothering oil.

Caddee warns Rhyonna, "Please, no risk taking. Be especially careful!"

4 - THE TRAP

RHYONNA APPRECIATES Caddee's worries. "I will be all right. My plan is to find the Junior Patrol and return for the Tawnyee's flying lesson. Tell my Mother Emma and Father Adair I'll help clean when I return."

In haste to fly, Rhyonna does not hear her best friend Caddee and the four Flyers shout, "Goodbye!"

Rhyonna sings:
Up I pull my wings.
Smoothly, they lift.
Down I push my wings.
I find the gray trail.
Through the air I glide,
Hovering by the buttercups,
Hanging by the creek,
I find the Junior Patrol.
Through high grasses I soar,
Spiraling the spikes of seeds,

Pivoting around spiders' webs,
I hear no rhythm of wings.
Into the sky, I climb.
Higher, higher,
Drifting with the wind,
Floating along the lake,
I see no Junior Patrol, no dusty trail.
I should rest,
So tired and so hot!

Rhyonna floats in the current of air into the Oak grove. Aha! Her favorite arum flower stands in the shade of the largest Oak tree. The purple arum will hold her cooling bath.

"Mmm! The sweetness is good."

A voice from above, the ancient sheegahshee spirit of the Oak, old Oakee, cautions, *"Faery Rhyonna, that arum is sour. This is not a plant."*

The engaging fragrance beckons Rhyonna and wills not to heed old Oakee's warning.

"In I leap. Wheeeeee!"

Rhyonna slows her wings and glides through the broad leaves to the pouch where the nectars collect.

Rhyonna sings:
Slip through the opening,
Glide into a wide pocket,
Spiral to the bottom,
My glow shines.

In the stale pouch, gray stains the arum walls. Sharp stinging hurts Rhyonna's mouth and nose. The flower holds soured air. Rhyonna is queasy, unable to move, and then fright shakes her.

"TRAPPED! HELP!" her shrills echo around the flower.

The opening to the outside world closes. The flower tips and then jerks up and down. Rhyonna slips in gray fluffed slime, which sticks to her. Smashing into the walls, Rhyonna tightly holds her wings, screaming.

"Kee-ggaan-n-n? Mo-om-mm e-e-e-e!"

In the scurry, Rhyonna pushes her knees and elbows tight against the wall edge to hold steady and protect her wings.

The trap stops, then tips upside down. Rhyonna grips tighter. The trap shakes and twists until Rhyonna slides down the slimy walls.

Down into a cold puddle of goop Rhyonna plunges. Her wings smash and crunch on cold clay. Musty mildew stings her nose and throat. Squirming and sliding, Rhyonna screams. "Fly! **Fly!**" Her wings are still, numbed.

Rhyonna pushes up from the goop onto her hands and knees. Circled around her stand bewildered Grayed Creatures. Then one knocks her flat on her stomach. Back into the sticky gray goop Rhyonna sinks. Then prickly feet squeeze her down. Her glow dims while her arms and legs thump heavily into the slime. Rhyonna's mind blurs, and her body numbs.

The Grayed Creatures grovel,
> *"See her shine."*
>> *"See her wings."*
>>> *"Zzuf, PLEASED."*

5 -THE LADYBUGS

GRAYED CREATURES with their hard claws pinch Rhyonna's arms and legs. To escape their hold, Rhyonna pulls and twists. Her delicate wings tear in her efforts to fly.

Their claws clamp tighter. Along a dark tunnel, the Creatures drag her.

Over and over, Rhyonna yells!

"HELP ME!"

Her cries echo and drown in the empty tunnels in the darkened caves.

The Grayed Creatures throw her into a dark room. Her wings crunch against the wall. Unsteadily shines her glow. Rhyonna tugs on her yellow dress that sticks to the wet clay. A bitter taste hangs in the humid cold.

When Rhyonna pushes up from the damp clay floor, dread rips through her.

Eyes stare from the dark, then piercing murmurs beat against the clay walls. This fear is unbearable.

Her faint glow reveals Ladybugs. Rhyonna holds her hands over her ears until the whimpering stops. "Ladybugs, you protect the BlackBerries." Rhyonna studies the fluff growing on their orange shells. "What happened?"

"You glow," notices one.

"You, a faery," mumbles another.

Rhyonna rises on her knees, pain throbbing through her wings. Carefully, to cause less harm, Rhyonna pushes up with her hands. Hurt streams in her eyes.

"Were you captured in the arum?"

One Ladybug comes forward. *"A fellow ladybug pointed the way to the green, fat sap-suckers. He said the aphids were the best he ate. When we rested on the grass, Grayed Creatures rushed from the ground and drove us in here."*

"The Grayed Creatures that Captain Keegan and Prince Blaire track."

"They keep us in the cold, damp dark," groans one.

"Feeding us BlackBerry syrup," whimpers another.

"That's where the syrup goes."

"The syrup makes us sick," sobs a Ladybug.

"Gray fluff grows," whines one.

"Think about home, your family, and friends."

"We lose memory," moans another.

"Remember, the Faeries honor and love you for protecting the BlackBerries from the awful sap-sucking aphids."

A crack breaks into the clay wall. Grayed Creatures slide acorn caps full of berry syrup into the room. From the syrup stings the odor of mildew. Rhyonna crawls in front of the acorns to block the Ladybugs.

"That's mildew. When it grows on the syrup, we get sick."

The aphid eaters shuffle to the syrup. They push Rhyonna and crawl over her to reach the bowls of poison. "Wait! Don't eat that!"

With their claws, the aphid eaters stuff the fluffed syrup into their mouths.

"STOP! You will die."

The Ladybugs do not listen. The syrup sticks to the fluff growing on their spotted shells. They slurp the syrup from each other. Sobbing, Rhyonna wilts to the floor.

The Protectors of the BlackBerry bushes, Eaters of the Aphids, the once spry Ladybugs, distort into Grayed Creatures, who steal from the village, the ones Captain Keegan with the Junior Patrol hunt.

"AGGGGHH!" Rhyonna screams until her throat is sore. Then Rhyonna repeats over and over, "Fluff will not eat me. Fluff will not eat me. Fluff - will - not - eat - me!" Until her sobs drown out the words.

The clay wall opens. A stick touches each fluffed clump. When a Ladybug resists, the probe goes to the next lump. The dazed are pulled through the slit. They follow without a fight. Eventually, all Ladybugs become the grayed, spore-making fluff.

Rhyonna's sobs turn into gulps of fear.

"I'm Brawny Rhyonna Faery, Flying Teacher for the Wee Flyers."

Rhyonna's mind hunts for her family. The face of her worried mother turns toward her. Rhyonna will never see her family again because of her hasty desire to find the Patrol. Rhyonna crumples into a ball, numbed with her burden.

Thick mildew smells enter the damp room. Grayed Creatures pinch Rhyonna. They drag her down a long tunnel. To guard her wings, Rhyonna arches her back and lifts up. The Grayed Creatures plunk her into another dark, damp room.

Rhyonna falls into a puddle of cold, sticky water. Pain keeps her from moving. On stale walls her glow flickers dark orange. Alone, lost, with her wings damaged, Rhyonna whimpers.

"Help m-e-e-e-e! Keegan, come get me!"

6 - CAVES

LOW SCRAPING and rustling sounds crowd the room. Spores wisp and whirl through the air as fluff crawls toward Rhyonna. A husky, muffled voice laughs.

"So, you FAERY!"

The grayed fluff leans forward into Rhyonna's face. Spores toss in and out of a gasping mouth, which muddle a gruff, offensive voice.

"Such a pretty!

"So glowing!

"So young!

"You be Zzuf!"

A high-pitched odor embitters the room; this fluff kills. Choking! Gagging! Fighting the infesting death, Rhyonna shivers. "What do you want?"

Sour thickens as Zzuf moves closer. The horrid fluff exhales roughly. A cloud of spores blow into Rhyonna's face. In bold refusal, Rhyonna seals her mouth. Spores splatter on her skin. Frantically, Rhyonna squashes the spores.

"You be Zzuf.

"We special.

"We parasitic.

"We eat sweet.

"You very sweet!"

Moving from the trembling glob, leaning on a wall, Rhyonna stiffens with defiance. "Where do you come from?"

Zzuf spits.

Rhyonna rubs the spores off. "Disgusting!"

"We always in caves.

"Waiting.

"We hornet queen."

A striped yellow and black shell of a hornet hangs covered with grayed, grasping fluff. Once-spirited wings bend with the blight. Rhyonna trembles. "You're a hornet?"

Clutched in a front leg is a stinger that Zzuf pokes. Rhyonna pushes tighter against the wall.

"You be me.

"We be you."

Rhyonna flares, "No! Never! I'm Brawny Rhyonna Faery, Flying Teacher for the Wee Flyers."

Contempt sputters from Zzuf's mouth.

"My darling, we Ladybugs.

"We sweet sap-suckers.

"We on berry bushes.

"We in berry syrup."

Slobbers drip from Zzuf's chin dropping to the wet floor. Fluff spreads across the clay, reaching.

"Now we are you!

"You spread us.

"Next eat everything."

Rhyonna stands upright and spits on Zzuf.

Expanding into a ball of long blurry hair, Zzuf tosses its stinger forward and bellows.

"You, tend us.

"We grow."

To the Grayed Creatures, Zzuf directs.

"Drag sweet faery to growing room."

Misery whirls around, as Rhyonna is dragged down a gloomy tunnel farther back into the caves.

Rhyonna can barely see; her glow fades brown. The creatures shove her into a murky room.

Without resisting, Rhyonna crumples, scared and hurt. The stale room is stacked with pieces of acorn shells and fluffed lumps of the once-Ladybugs. In dread, Rhyonna cries.

After a long, tearful, struggle Rhyonna sobs, "I will never be this ugly parasite." Digging into the damp clay, Rhyonna firmly rubs clay into the fluff, which grasps onto her arms, legs, dress, and face. Rhyonna wipes her fears off.

Refusing to surrender to her doom, Rhyonna lifts up. Slowly onto her hands then to her knees, not to hurt her wings, which hang limp. Carefully, tenderly, Rhyonna moves her crunched wings behind her while kneeling. Awkwardly balancing, Rhyonna searches the room and notices a dark, muggy puddle of water. Rhyonna crawls to the watery reflection.

Her weak orange glow mirrors brown hair full of clay, her face dirty, yellow dress torn, and her tattered wings. Rhyonna's eyes fill with gloom. Refusing despair, Rhyonna peers into the murky puddle and envisions hope for herself, her friends, and her family.

Rhyonna searches the puddle. Her Father Adair, Keeper of the BlackBerry bushes, clips moldy leaves from stems and hands them to her Mother Emma and the helpers. They carry the soured leaf clippings and toss them into a hole. The healer pours garlic oil over the wilted grayed foliage while the helpers push dirt on top of the fluffy mess.

After watching a long while, Rhyonna bends with exhaustion. Not giving up, Rhyonna again focuses on reflections.

Rhyonna yells, "Mom! Dad! The hideous parasite eats anything. It eats me."

Mother Emma listens for a second and then continues with the cleaning. Her mother fades.

Desperately, Rhyonna peers into the murky puddle. "Keegan! Keegan! Where are you?"

Deep into the syrupy puddle searches Rhyonna. By a creek, Keegan sits slouched, absorbed into the spray from the waterfall. Seeing his fears Rhyonna lovingly reaches to touch his blond hair.

"Keegan, come get me."

He looks up. "Rhyonna, where are you?"

Her hand stretches to caress his concerned face. "My wings are hurt! The fluff, the gray . . . "

Horror grips and blocks her vision, causing Keegan's image to fade into the murk. Her glow fades with sorrow. Rhyonna slumps into the broken acorn shells. Fluff reaches for her. Rhyonna yells at the horror, "I will survive. Never will I be Zzuf!"

Again, searching the syrupy puddle Rhyonna yells, "Fish! Fish! Help me!"

The muddy puddle reveals ripples on the lake. Rhyonna looks deep into the ripples. Her voice streams into the water. "Fish, come get me."

Rhyonna waits impatiently. The water swirls.

* * *

7 - THE MESSAGE

THE FINS OF FISH SOOTHE with "shh, shh!" He floats in the rich emerald mosses, listening, searching. *"Friend, where?"*

"I'm t r a p p e d i n a c a v e!"

Pain thrusts through Rhyonna's neck.

"O U C H . . . o u c h!"

Long claws dig into the soft skin on Rhyonna's neck. Not afraid of the fluffed shell, Rhyonna tightly squeezes her neck and shoulders together, resisting. Zzuf pinches deeper. Rhyonna stands up.

"You ugly sour, let go!"

Wrathful spores sputter; Rhyonna wipes them off.

"You keep damp!

"We grow!"

In loathing, Rhyonna grabs an acorn filled with syrupy slime and flings at Zzuf. Spitting spores,

Zzuf huffs through the puddle of murky mud out the opening of the room.

"I'll get out of here!" Rhyonna yells after the blurred fluff.

Searching for Fish's reflections in the muddy pool, Rhyonna whimpers holding laments. Waiting helplessly because of her desired to go alone and find the Junior Patrol.

Rhyonna sees Fish as he breaks the surface of the water. He swims to a royal green Dragonfly perched on a rock facing the warming sun, humming. Rhyonna gasps, "Majestic, my Dragonfly!" Fish hears her cry.

Fish watches Majestic while he hums, gently flapping his wings up and down.

"Eater of my Baby Nymphs, why do you look?"

Fish carefully balances in the shallow water. *"Help, friend!"*

Majestic rotates on the rock facing Fish, demanding, *"Of whom do you speak?"*

"Rhyonna!" Fish bursts out.

Majestic's eyes challenge Fish. *"Rhyonna, my favorite. Yes! Rhyonna. I see her this day."*

"Hopeless, sullen." Fish coughs concern.

"Go on, for Rhyonna's sake."

"Sick, worried." Fish chokes in grief.

"Yes, go on!"

"Trapped. Helpless!" Shutters Fish.

Horror grips Dragonfly. *"Rhyonna trapped!"* Majestic pops his wings. *"Eater of my Baby Nymphs, yes! I will carry the message up the creek to the Faeries for Brawny Rhyonna, whom I love."*

"Nymphs safe." Fish carefully backs into the lake.

Rhyonna shouts into the reflection in the puddle, "Help comes!"

Majestic stretches his mighty legs. He crawls higher on the rock. Long wings swing up to pull the air. They sweep down with a deep pushing swish. The hum of Majestic pops into a whiz. Up into the sky he lifts and disappears.

Horrid fluff stretches across the floor Rhyonna splashes it with water. The parasite flattens and stops its grasp. Rhyonna peers into the puddle to watch Majestic, who soars up the creek to the BlackBerry bushes.

Rhyonna sighs. "Keegan will find me."

By the creek near the waterfall, Majestic finds Teacher Caddee with the wee students. As he lands on the sand, his wings *pop!*

Rhyonna watches Caddee turn to the Dragonfly calling, "Majestic?"

Hopeful, Rhyonna wipes her fears from her eyes to keep the image. Caddee and the wee students run to the Dragonfly. Majestic lifts his wings to flash alert.

Caddee shouts, "Where is Rhyonna? Are the Tawnyee Flyers with her?"

Rhyonna gasps, "The Tawnyee Flyers with me?"

Rhyonna dizzily drops into horror. Zzuf has them. Rhyonna sobs into regret. The Flyers flew from the village. All Rhyonna had to do was bring the four Flyers along to follow the gray dust.

Caddee's voice brings Rhyonna back to the damp caves. "Were the Tawnyee Flyers with her?"

Majestic pops, *"NO! No Flyers, nothing of them."*

Clutching the mud, Rhyonna wails. "The Tawnyee Flyers gone. All this anguish, because I wanted praise as the best flyer in the village."

Trembling, Rhyonna struggles to keep their reflections. Caddee walks closer to Majestic, who continues. *"Moments ago, I got a message from Fish, who saw Rhyonna in the water ripples. Fish said Rhyonna had gray mud all over, her glow was sullen, and wings limp and fluffy."*

"My WINGS!"

Through her regrets, steadying, Rhyonna stares into the puddle and listen.

"Did Fish say where?"

"Fish said 'trapped.' Then Rhyonna disappeared into a ripple."

"The clay caves by the lake?" Caddee asks.

Majestic buzzes, *"Right, the gray caves. On my rounds I'll watch for Rhyonna and the Flyers."*

Majestic ascends into the air and rushes down the creek.

Caddee shouts to him, "I'll tell Rhyonna's parents. Our Queen will send Captain Keegan and the Junior Patrol to search for her."

Up the creek, Teacher Caddee flies with her wee students, fluttering as fast as they can.

Rhyonna gazes into the forbidding clay, bellowing her guilt into the silent wall. The wet clay muffles any appeal. The fluff reaches for her. Fear stings her eyes; Rhyonna squints to hold back weeping.

Opening her eyes, Rhyonna observes a movement in the clay wall. The fluff jerks. Probing feelers poke through a small hole.

8 - THE DARE

KNEELING ON THE DAMP CLAY, Rhyonna softens her breathing and observes the fluff moving. Only the *drip, drip, drip* of water fills the room.

A tiny brown ant pushes back the fluff and crawls through a small hole in the wall. This creature scurries along the top of the fluff while another ant crawls out. They cut and push the gray fluff through the opening to a third and fourth ant. These ants place the horrid sap-suckers on the BlackBerry bushes. Now they spread Zzuf into their colony.

Taking a deep breath, Rhyonna stretches as large as possible and thrusts in front of the ants.

"Stay, or I'll tell Zzuf you steal it."

The four scurry back into the hole. Rhyonna grabs the back leg of the last one. "I know who you are, thieves."

Feelers appear, then four heads. Rhyonna releases the ant's leg.

"Who speaks to us?" asks a cunning voice.

"I am Rhyonna Faery, Flying Teacher for the Wee Flyers."

The four ants climb into the cave. *"You threaten us, the Scouts to our Queen Floree?"*

"Listen to me. Zzuf is evil."

They stroke the fluff.

One drones, *"We do not think so. We love it."*

"Zzuf will turn you into gray fluff. It needs helpers to keep its parasitic self alive."

One moves closer, *"You look like a faerrrry."*

A second scorns, *"Use your wings."*

A third mocks, *"Fly out the opening."*

The fourth scoffs, *"Where is your bright glow?"*

Rhyonna's anger swells. "I'm trapped. My wings are injured so I cannot fly. I eat mushrooms and my glow dims. Notice how the fluff grows on me."

The four ants touch Rhyonna with their feelers. They pull back.

One asks, *"What do you want?"*

"I need to go through your tunnel to the sun."

One smirks, *"We don't think so."*

The four ants retreat into the hole, smoothing clay over it. Rhyonna yanks the clay from the opening.

"This parasite eats sugar, your favorite food. Zzuf, that fluff you hold, plans to eat all the sugar everywhere! It eats me, you, whoever likes sugar!"

One ponders, *"Eat us?*

Another says, *"That's not pleasant."*

Their feelers pat each other's.

The next agrees, *"Okay, we will."*

The last warns, *"First we ask Our Queen Floree."*

They leave, packing clay back into the hole.

Finding a small mushroom and picking the soggy sponge, Rhyonna silently chews. Her brown glow exaggerates the shadows. Exhausted Rhyonna watches the hole for any movement. This hole is her life. The ants have one minute, then Rhyonna climbs through the hole.

Shuffled scraping interrupts and enters the room. Rhyonna's glow is too dim to see clearly. The loathing frightful Zzuf stoops and sputters a heavy, damp cloud on her. Standing, Rhyonna faces the souring fluff, saying nothing, shielding her mouth and eyes with her hands.

Zzuf chuckles.

"Little creatures love me.

"Carry me inside anthill.

"Helpers! Sugar eaters.

"We are ants.

"We spread."

Zzuf's laughter throws exploding spores toward Rhyonna, who turns away. When Zzuf leaves and drags through the tunnel, bits of blurred fluff cling to the walls, making Zzuf clumsy.

While the shuffle of Zzuf disappears into the hollow tunnel, Rhyonna scrapes clean wet clay from the wall and smashes the spores on her arms and her fraying dress. The fluff expands onto Rhyonna's wings, digging into the fibers.

Rhyonna sobs into dirty hands, "I will squash this sour. I caused this harm to my wings. I should have helped Caddee. My Tawnyee Flyers just wanted to fly with me."

9 - ESCAPE

A DAINTY WIGGLE of fluff growing on the wall alerts Rhyonna. As four ants slide through the hole, Rhyonna feels gentle pats from their feelers.

"Our Queen Floree gives permission," admires one. *"I am Scout Bryn."*

"Our Queen wants to talk to you," esteems another. *"Scout Neddy here."*

"Our Floree is interested in Zzuf. Scout Rue here."

"We lead you through our Colony. Scout Fay here."

The four look, talk and move like each other, the same and sisters. Busily, they enlarge the hole. They crawl through the opening, one looks back, *"Are you coming?"*

Reaching through the opening, Rhyonna tries to push up into a dark tunnel.

"The wall is too steep."

"With your hands and feet. Pull and push, crawl up."

"I must protect my wings."

"That's why six legs are better."

"My glow is too low to see anything."

"That is why we have feelers."

"Use your hands to feel the notches."

With her fingers, Rhyonna finds the notches the ants carved. Holding her wings tight, Rhyonna drags her tired, hurt body through the hole into the tunnel. Peering into darkness, bright colors dance in Rhyonna's eyes. The stillness rings in her ears.

In the tunnel blows a faint breeze tinted with meadow fragrance. Her feet find and step into the notches that go straight up the tunnel. Pulling upwards slowly and carefully, Rhyonna cautiously protects her wings.

One guide informs, *"Three of us will climb above you. Scout Neddy will direct from below."* Feelers pleasantly tap directing Rhyonna's arms and legs. The taps feel like the softness of a wee faery's hand.

Then the tunnel opens. Rhyonna lifts through an opening into a chamber. The warmth of a beach in summer heat welcomes her. Peppermint flows through the air, calming.

Feelers softy touch Rhyonna. A pleasing, loving voice speaks, *"Greetings, Faery. Our cocoons are buried in the sand in this chamber. Helpers moved the sand here from the beach, grain by grain."*

Rhyonna, with her low orange glow, observes the smoothed sand. Ants have determination. Once Rhyonna watched the ants carry small pebbles.

The guides lead Rhyonna to another hole. Protecting her battered wings and with much effort, Rhyonna pulls into a tunnel and slowly climbs up another notched ladder. Nothing like flying, her body is heavier than a rock and not agile. Intently Rhyonna copies Lender the Lizard, climbing his rock while always protecting her damaged wings.

Touching an edge, Rhyonna pulls through into another chamber. Lavender, lemon, and rose aroma follows swells of air. Jingling, low buzzing, and faint padding play as music.

A soft, caring voice invites, *"Greetings, Dear Faery. Our babies mature in this chamber. Nurses turn and clean the pupae."*

Before Rhyonna can comment, her guides' feelers move her to another hole in the wall. The ant colony is deep and complex. Beyond exhaustion,

Rhyonna forces herself to climb. Entering another chamber, the fragrances of dried sage, orange, and thyme flood over her.

Rhyonna sighs, "HOME!"

A generous voice offers, *"Greetings, Faery. This is the storage chamber for our seeds."*

Rhyonna sniffs back regret and rubs sorrow from her eyes with her soiled hands.

Into a flat, wide tunnel with no walls, the four guides move Rhyonna. Busy ants carrying objects curiously bump, push, and tap her. Through this maze of rushing workers, the four guides shift Rhyonna this way and that to protect her.

Through the tunnel, the voices echo, *"Faery?"* *"Faery?"* *"Faery!"* *"FAERY!"*

Tired by the busy momentum and her own weariness, Rhyonna attempts to lie down on the clay floor. The worried guides hold Rhyonna standing.

"Strength," advises one.

"This is the last chamber," encourages another.

The four guides turn Rhyonna into a long hall into the sweet impact of wheat, rye, oats, and barley grass. Instantly Rhyonna is home and fluttering across the Meadow of Flowers with Majestic. Investigating taps cause Rhyonna to twist abruptly. The pain in her wings streaks through the moment, Rhyonna returns to the ant colony.

In a background of soft laughter, a kind voice speaks, *"Greetings, Faery. These rooms hold the different nurseries for our children: gathers, nurses, guards, scouts, Queens, and the males . . ."*

Rhyonna interrupts the voice. "Please, I'm tired, I will collapse."

The four guides hold Rhyonna while the voice continues. *"The babies want to touch you. They hear talk about Faeries flying at the lake. Your wings are curious to them."*

Rhyonna pleads again, "Please, do not touch me, especially my wings. Children, a horrid fluff grows on me and will eat you also."

A sympathetic voice says, *"We have protections."*

The soft touches tickle Rhyonna, who laughs. Then the children laugh in an ant's way. For an instant, Rhyonna is with the Wee Ones, snuggling in Dandelion.

"Your children give me hope. Thank you!"

Sobbing guilt spreads into Rhyonna, "Ants are so caring." With kindness, a nurse pats Rhyonna.

Her guides direct her into an empty, steep, diagonal tunnel going down. With gentleness, the guides hold Rhyonna up. Into a large open chamber, they lead her where sharp, spicy grass whiffs through the air. Rhyonna is stopped. The squashy, muffled scraping, and thumping that filled the chamber drowns into silent waiting.

Tapped firmly, Rhyonna straightens. These taps from the guides say, *"You are here!"*

In the darkness, Rhyonna steadies for what seem hours then startled by gentle pats.

"Brawny Faery Rhyonna, I am Aide Erstwood, our Queen Floree's Aide of Messages. I bring all news from the colony to Queen Floree. Honored Faery. Speak directly to our Queen."

A noble voice requests, *"Bring the faery closer."* Aide Erstwood moves Rhyonna into the center of the chamber. Thick earthy odors enhance Rhyonna's exhaustion, and anguish causes her glow to fade.

10 - QUEEN FLOREE

THE OFFICIAL VOICE of the Aide Erstwood announces, *"Our Queen Floree. Escorted by Scout Ants: Bryan, Fay, Neddy, and Rue; Brawny Faery Rhyonna greet Queen of our Colony by the Lake of the Oaks."*

Rhyonna curtseys to a huge dark shape. Her low glow only reveals shadows of orange and black. "Queen Floree, I am honored to be in your colony. I am Brawny Rhyonna, Teacher of Flying for the Wee Flyers of the BlackBerry Village by Oak Lake."

Queen Floree touches Rhyonna's face, distinct and discreetly. Then the Queen taps the fluff that grows on Rhyonna's skin, dress, and wings. Even though her small, frail body shakes, Rhyonna forces herself to stand steady. Her legs weaken. Rhyonna will fall to the ground any second.

Then scraping and rubbing disturbs the intense quiet of the chamber. The soft voice of Queen Floree asks, *"Brawny Rhyonna Faery, my Scouts tell me you were in gray caves and that you say they are full of fluff that plans to eat us."*

Queen Floree denies the certainty. Rhyonna tightens every muscle to firm her stand. "Your Majesty Queen Floree, fluff grows everywhere."

"My dear, there is nothing for mold to grow on in the caves."

Queen Floree is not alarmed. Determined, Rhyonna persists or the ants will die with her. "Your Majesty, Zzuf is a hornet's shell covered with fluff."

"NO! Queen Hornet. We made an agreement about my place and her place. We are to honor each other's."

A sticky, earthy scent overwhelms and is and suppressive. Trembling, Rhyonna's head thumps. "Your Majesty, Zzuf is a parasite that grows all over the hornet shell. Zzuf can hardly talk or move. It carries the hornet's stinger. It breathes spores that spread fluff on the damp walls."

An odor of rotting spreads over the earthy smells. *"This cannot be. I talked to the hornet when she entered the caves to build her nest. She was so happy and alert. Bright!"*

Sharp resistance spreads around the room. Rhyonna challenges, "Well, the fluff ate the hornets, just as it eats me."

The busy shuffling drowns into silent awareness. Death enters the chamber. *"What does the Zzuf eat?"* confronts the Queen.

Rhyonna stands straighter, directly to Queen Floree says, "Zzuf eats anything sweet, sugars. The parasite is in your colony, eating you."

Rhyonna hears agitated movements, then a thick peppery odor swirls around the room.

"Faery Rhyonna, how did this come to be?"

Unsteady, rocking back and forth, Rhyonna explains. "Zzuf, a parasitic mold, used hornets to capture Ladybugs. Eating moldy BlackBerry syrup the Ladybugs turn into fluff, who is Zzuf. They leave the cave and spread spores on everything."

One guide says, *"Yes, our Queen Floree, we see the fluff."*

One confirms, *"Fluff is on our sweet sap-suckers."*

"Zzuf said it is pleased to find your ants steal from the caves, it spreads into your colony faster."

The offensive pepper thickens through the chamber and chokes Rhyonna. Queen Floree bursts into rage. *"This cannot be. We have a repellent we rub on our bodies."*

Overcome, Rhyonna falls to the floor. The four guides help her up; Rhyonna leans against them. Coughing Rhyonna forces more words. "Zzuf spread to the ants, to me, on and on and on. Zzuf plans to eat ours and yours and the others!"

"NO! Faery Rhyonna."

The four stroke Rhyonna as their good friend.

"I must go to my village. Four of my wee Flyers search for me. Zzuf might have them."

For what seems like minutes, the only sounds are Rhyonna's rasping breath and pounding heart. Then the chamber explodes.

"AaaaGGggghhh," bellows Queen Floree. *"That's what grows on us!"*

Into a dark hallway, the four rush Rhyonna.

"Go this way."

"Hurry!"

"Climb up this tunnel."

"You will see the light."

The four shove Rhyonna up into a long, dark tunnel. Below is the scurry of the ants and grief-stricken moans of Queen Floree. The fluff eats the colony.

"Brawny Faery, catch the notches. Pull."

Upward Rhyonna edges slowly because of her exhaustion and the need to protect her wings. Ahead is sunlight. The four push one last time. Rhyonna pulls through an entrance while rocks tumble into the tunnel.

Rhyonna is out and shouts down.

"Good-bye friends, your kindness will be remembered."

One reminds, *"Little time!"*

One ant urges, *"Go fast!"*

Another asks, *"Remember your guides, Scouts Bryn, Neddy, Rue, and Fay."*

The last one requests, *"Tell the Faeries about us."*

Rhyonna crawls onto the mound of small rocks, carefully tending her wilted wings. Sunshine glares, blurring her eyes. The face of a large ant with claws for a mouth stares at her. When touched by long feelers, Rhyonna hardens and holds her breath. This ant is twice the size of the Scouts. *"Brawny Faery Rhyonna, nice to see you. This is I, Guard Prior."*

"Yes, why yes! The guard I met on the hill when I followed the line."

The giant guard reverently pats Rhyonna. *"Faery, you remember Guard Prior."*

Hearing the soft words, Rhyonna relaxes. "Where am I?"

"On the east bank of the Lake of the Oaks."

"Guard Prior, will you help me?"

"Please wait. I place the stones back to keep the air flowing into the colony. The others need the air to breathe."

When the guard ant finishes, Rhyonna gently wraps her arms around the giant to hold herself up. "I'm ready, Guard Prior. Walk me slowly."

Although filled with pain, Rhyonna leans against the giant for balance, concentrating on walking without hurting her wings. "Thank-you, Guard Prior!"

"We go slow, over the small rocks,

"through thistles who poke here and there."

The giant's walk is the rhythm of the butterflies as they float.

"Now, through the grasses,

"to here the edge of the lake."

Rhyonna's wings hang silent, not pumping up or down. Her pain is horrendous. Worse is Rhyonna's grief for the Tawnyee Flyers.

"Brawny Rhyonna, you are strong. Courageous!"

"The horrid Zzuf may have my four Flyers. They followed me."

"The Scouts will search on their outings."

With her front legs, Guard Prior hugs and lowers Rhyonna to the sand in the sunshine by the water. Rhyonna smiles at the giant.

"Thank you for your kindness and thoughts."

"Please, Brawny Faery Rhyonna, remember Guard Prior to the wee faeries."

"This I will do, Guard Prior."

11 - MAJESTIC

RHYONNA SQUINTS as sunshine flashes into her eyes. Her hands shadow the brilliance. The silhouette of Guard Prior walks up the hill to the colony. Through the gleams of light, Rhyonna admires the giant's agility. Guard Prior is gracefully strong, reassuring. Rhyonna now understands walking on and under the ground, which ants enjoy every day. Queen Floree's colony is like her village. The ants love and help each other.

Shivering, while thinking of the horrid fluff, Rhyonna yells, "I will never be Zzuf!"

The hot air resting on the ground collects around her. Rhyonna carefully cuddles her wings. The musical humming of others in the air sings welcome. Each breath dries her mouth and lungs. The healthy heat wilts, shrinks, and dries the fluff.

Rhyonna crawls to the lake. In the mirror reflection, Rhyonna faces herself. Fluffed patches stick here and there on her arms, legs, hands, face, and hair. Her once-yellow dress is grayed with dying fluff. Her greatest sorrow is her tattered wings, which hang limp with fluff clutching into them.

This vile parasite, this infectious has her. Rhyonna shutters. In time, spores will sputter from her mouth. Dread stiffens her. Frantically, Rhyonna screams through the pain. "HELP! **HELP ME!**"

Rhyonna pounds the sand hard, then harder, wailing. "I am to blame! My wings damaged! The Tawnyee Flyers lost! Zzuf spreads to the others!"

Rhyonna stares into the vastness of guilt.

Busy flies quiet their buzz and peer at her. Rhyonna sees their concern. Watching, the others come with respect for her. Their songs and music surrounds Rhyonna and opens her hope.

Rhyonna screams, "**I LIVE.**"

Cherishing fills, acceptance floods, and appreciation grows. Snuggling into the warmth, Rhyonna is lulled to sleep.

"Rhyonna. Rhyonna! Wake up!"
Two feelers and two legs shake her.

"*Rhyonna, I search for you. Fish told me that you are in trouble. I see you here.*"

"Majestic! You found me."

Rhyonna struggles to sit up, wanting to hug Dragonfly only stops the fluff will spread to her dear friend. Gently swinging his wings, Majestic maintains a soothing breeze. "*Rhyonna, what is the gray fluff on you?*"

Concern in the mighty gold-green Dragonfly's eyes alarms Rhyonna. "Parasitic mold. It also grows inside me. This horrid fluff may get on you."

Majestic stops his buzzing and flapping of wings. He checks Rhyonna's fluffed and torn wings. "*My life is too short for the fluff to hurt my flight.*"

Whimpers catch in her throat. Rhyonna wilts back into the sand. "Majestic, I may never fly."

Majestic crawls closer to Rhyonna and crouches to the sand. "*You were in the caves.*"

"This horrid fluff, which calls itself Zzuf, lives there. I escaped with the help of the ants, I climbed through their colony."

"*I will fly you to your village. Teacher Caddee says the Tawnyee Flyers search for you.*"

Rhyonna's pains stifle her voice. Finally her tears break the hold. "I caused all of this."

Majestic stares at Rhyonna, *"You found a horror; now rid of it with help from your friends."*

"Thank you, Majestic, you are my best friend."

Slowly Rhyonna pushes herself up and crawls close to Majestic. While Rhyonna pulls herself up and leans against the giant, he stands supportive. Then slowly, attentive to her wings, Rhyonna crawls up onto Majestic's shiny gold-green back. Rhyonna slides between his strong wings and nestles into Majestic. Her arms hug her best friend. The sun flashes on the blues and yellows woven into the lace of his wings. Rhyonna is safe.

Eagerness for home rushes at her, "I'm ready."

"Balanced, Rhyonna?"

"Yes, fly slow, Majestic."

Majestic pushes up with his long legs. His mighty lace wings open and stretch across the air, pulling. Then his wings close around the moving air, pushing down, whizzing. Up flies the giant.

The air whistles, pressed between the powerful pulls and pushes. The wings of the giant hum the low tone that Rhyonna loves. Around Majestic, cool air flows and presses against Rhyonna's face and refreshes her. The flight of the giant is power and confidence.

The reflections from the lake glisten in the dancing wind. The trees around the lake stand firm. With the speed of Majestic, the colors of the flowers blend into a rainbow. The comfort from the push and pull, the thrill of flying, embraces Rhyonna. Her friend, the mighty giant Dragonfly, carries Rhyonna to safety.

12 - HOME

MAJESTIC LANDS outside the BlackBerry Village on the beach along the creek. *"You are in loving lands. I leave to watch my places."* Buzzing and popping, Majestic ascends whizzing into the sky.

All the wee Faeries from the village scurry from under the BlackBerry bushes. They fly as fast as they can toward Rhyonna, who motions them back yelling, "Don't fly to me."

Struggling to get her breath, Rhyonna shouts, "The fluff on me will make you sick."

To the ground Rhyonna falls.

Frantic, four Tawnyee Flyers flutter faster.

Again, Rhyonna shouts, "You will get the parasite. Listen to me! Stay back!"

When almost to Rhyonna, together Darren Gale, Beti Kacie, Evan Roy, and Princess Lessie Shelly shout, "Rhyonna is back!"

Rhyonna sighs, "You are home?"

"A spider helped us," answers Darren Gale.

No lecture; they are safe. Rhyonna longs to hug them, instead covers her mouth, and breathes down into the sand to protect the Flyers from any spores that escape into the air.

The Flyers stop and stare at Rhyonna's tattered, fluffed, and grayed wings.

The adult villagers stop, stunned by the damage to her and the grayed fluff. The birds, frogs, toads, insects, small rodents, flowers, trees, and butterflies, all the others stop still.

Her Father Adair kneels by her, his eyes cloud with tears. "Rhyonna, what happened?"

"Dad, don't hug me. The fluff grows on me that spoils the BlackBerries, the syrup, and eats me."

Rhyonna shakes with trauma. Her Mother Emma picks Rhyonna up and cuddles her.

"Mother, don't hold me."

Emma Mother does not listen, repeating. "My daughter, what happened to you?"

"I flew to find the Junior Patrol tracking the gray trail. I stopped to take a bath in my favorite arum flower. Only it was a trap. Grayed Creatures carried me to a hornet called Zzuf, which is moldy fluff.

The horrid parasite said it eats everything sweet. It spit spores on me until I became infested."

The villagers grumble in disgust and move back.

"The Ladybugs are the Grayed Creatures. Zzuf eats them. They carry this fluffy mold, which is Zzuf to eat our berries, then us."

Rhyonna can say no more; her nightmare hits and becomes shock. Her eyes blur, mouth dries, and body shivers. Rhyonna mumbles, "I need sunshine. The fluff dries . . ."

Mother carries Rhyonna to the burning heat of the sun. Healer Leanna moves forward and offers Rhyonna water and a flower from the primrose to chew. She examines Rhyonna's skin, hair, and wings.

"Your wings have the most damage. You fell on them?"

"I did," whimpers Rhyonna. "The Grayed Creatures dragged me down tunnels and tossed me into a wet, moldy room."

Rhyonna hesitates, and then asks, "Will I fly?" Her voice drowns in worries about being the Flying Teacher for the Wee Flyers.

"Flying will take time. First, we get you free of this fluff and your wings healed."

"Where are Keegan, Prince Blaire, and Caddee?"

"Caddee told us that Majestic, your Dragonfly, said you were in the gray caves by the Lake of the Oaks," Queen Tanya answers. "They left some time ago to search for you, without consent from the Elders. We have great concern."

"The Senior Patrol searches for them. They left yesterday," King Grady adds.

Rhyonna shudders, "Zzuf could have them in the caves, just as it caught me. I thought only of the fun of the chase. Now look at me."

The Tawnyee Flyers settle quietly, looking embarrassed and awkward.

Queen Tanya comforts, "Please, Rhyonna, what's important, now, is that you are home."

"What happened in the caves?" asks King Grady.

"Our syrup grows fluff on others who are captured. The fluff grows from spores; it eats into my wings."

With alarm, the villagers pull back from Rhyonna. The birds, frogs, toads, all insects, small rats and mice, all animals, flowers, trees, and butterflies hush in fear.

"I washed with clean mud and ate mushrooms to keep sugar out of my body. The mushrooms dimmed my glow."

Concern irritates the eyes of those listening.

"Ants stole the fluff. I told them that fluff would eat them."

"That's why no ants are around," realizes King Grady.

"Zzuf saw them stealing and laughed, saying, 'We the ants, then the others.'"

Fearful, the villagers listen, distressed.

"King Grady, the ants are busy in their colony. Queen Floree said they had no protection."

King Grady steps closer, "You had an audience with the ant queen?"

"Queen Floree said the ants want to help us." Rhyonna pauses looking at the villages. "If she is still alive. The Queen let me climb out the colony to tell others about Zzuf."

The villagers talk all at once. Rhyonna understands their fear and anger. The ants put the sap-suckers on the village BlackBerry flowers to steal the sweet sap.

Queen Tanya quiets them. "Let Rhyonna speak."

"Queen Floree smelled of dry, spicy grasses mingling in the warmth of the day's sun. The ant colony is like our village, helpful to each other."

"Why would ants help?" King Grady asks.

"Queen Floree was outraged. Zzuf wants her ants to spread the fluff to eat all others."

Animals, birds, insects, flowers, trees, and the wind rustle anguish and disgust.

Queen Tanya announces, "Rhyonna needs to rest. Tomorrow, the Elders will decide what to do about Queen Floree and the ants."

The village Seamstresses bring a dry grass carrier to Rhyonna. Her Father Adair lifts her into the chair. The Village Elders fly Rhyonna to Dandelion, which waits in the sunshine. While the Elders hold the woven platform close to the strongest flower, Rhyonna crawls onto soft petals. Dandelion snuggles Rhyonna. A tart spice rolls into the air and enlivens; Rhyonna is home.

The King and Queen with the villagers and Tawnyee Flyers flutter to their homes. Mother Emma and Healer Leanna stay to tend Rhyonna.

Healer Leanna hands garlic water to Rhyonna to drink. The heat burns her mouth and makes her eyes and nose sting. The fire burns in her stomach. Then Healer Leanna washes Rhyonna with the garlic oil. Afterwards, she spreads a thick garlic ointment on the soured spots. The heat warms the irritations. Then she rubs the oil from the evening primrose all over Rhyonna's skin.

Lastly, Healer Leanna washes Rhyonna's hair with soap weed and rubs crushed garlic on her scalp. Then she coats Rhyonna's hair with the evening primrose oil and combs out dead fluff.

Finally, with thinned garlic oil and the softest of hand, Rhyonna's wings are soothed. With the most gentleness, Healer Leanna binds the wings with spider silk to keep the wings set.

Too exhausted to complain, Rhyonna remains calm during these discomforts. The fluff begins to wilt in the soured spots.

For Rhyonna, Mother Emma gathers meadow pollens and flower nectar to eat and drink. Her Mother holds and hums to Rhyonna, who fills with love.

As the night approaches, Dandelion wraps strong green leaves around Rhyonna and snuggles her gently. Rhyonna dreams of play in the Meadow of Flowers with the Tawnyee Flyers, her beloved Keegan, best friend Caddee, and Prince Blaire.

13 - SPIDER ERWINA

DANDELION OPENS to the warming sun. Rhyonna awakes and watches yellow flowers pull open to praise the light.

"Oh, Dandelion, what a perfect day. I am ALIVE! I am home! Hello, sun. Hello, sky. Good morning, trees. Hello, singing birds. Hello, wind. Good morning, dancing flowers. I fly with you soon."

Rhyonna raises her arms as if to dive into the sky, stretches, and sings:

As my Dandelion opens,
Sunshine streams across velvet petals.
The light of the sun warms me,
Brightly I shine polished by Dandelion.
As my Dandelion opens,
The morning light flickers
And dances on me and reflects my joy.
The pinks of the rising sun ignite my cheeks.
The greens of the earth glisten in my eyes.
As my Dandelion opens,

I gently pick the sparkles from the dewdrops.
I balance them on my ears.
Then I scatter their light on my hair,
Which flows around me like air streams.
As my Dandelion opens,
I savor her crunchy pollen.
I relish her zestful, tart flavor.
Her flowers' spicy fragrance clears my head.
As my Dandelion opens,
I have her strength and boldness.
I love and appreciate Dandelion.

Rhyonna slowly chews the spicy pollen, savoring the taste. A yellow and black butterfly flitters toward her, followed by three others. They float here, there, and then they settle next to Rhyonna on the opened flowers of Dandelion.

"Rufus, how nice to see you."

"Absorbing, dearest Faery?"

"My wings are damaged," whines Rhyonna.

"Grieving flying?"

Rhyonna points to white fluff. "Here on my wings."

"Wanting, knowing, dearest Faery?"

"A mutant fluff soured me as it does the others."

Rufus pulls his wings up, as do the other three butterflies. *"Snowing winter?"*

"No, summer horror. Zzuf, a horrid parasitic mold spreads into our realms. Stay away from the fluff. The spores eat anything sweet."

"Terrifying, telling friends, stopping blow."

Up from the Dandelion, Rufus and his three friends bound and flitter away through the Meadow. Rhyonna sees fear and tension in the up and down of their flight. The butterflies disappear into the flicking light of the trees. Deep despair throbs in Rhyonna, who slumps into the comfort of Dandelion.

Along the trees, Rhyonna glimpses her Mother Emma and Healer Leanna flying from the village. They escort the Tawnyee Flyers to Dandelion. The four Flyers land on open flowers around Rhyonna and giggle. Their darling innocent faces smile at her. Love shines as warm as the sun and fills

Rhyonna, who sends her love back to the four Flyers.

"Mother, are Keegan, Caddee, and Prince Blaire back?"

"No. Queen Tanya sent more Senior Patrol to search for them."

"All because I want to be the best flyer. My selfishness damaged my wings, now my friends are lost."

Mother Emma cuddles Rhyonna. "You are and will stay be the best flyer. No stress! You are to rest."

Healer Leanna patiently unwraps the spider webbing from Rhyonna's wings. Carefully, slowly, she spreads fresh garlic and primrose oil over the soured spots. "The spots heal."

The four Flyers look at Rhyonna with perfect adoration, so full of hope. With affection, Rhyonna studies the four, who squirm.

"The Elders and Queen and King will keep my flying lessons?"

"Rhyonna, healing is first."

To the four Rhyonna asks, "So Tawnyee Flyers, why were you out in the forest after I left? You were to help Teacher Caddee clean up the dust."

A long silence flows around Dandelion. Mother Emma and Healer Leanna sit on flowers and wait for their story. Rhyonna tenderly surveys the four.

Darren Gale offers, "Don't be angry. We wanted to follow the gray trail and find you and Captain Keegan!"

"So did I." Rhyonna smiles kindness to them.

Darren Gale continues, "Rhyonna, you know me. I convinced the others. And, especially Princess Lessie Shelly, she would tattle to the Queen and King after we left."

Princess Lessie Shelly flutters around. "I would tell because I wanted to come."

"I was easy to convince." Evan Roy says, "I wanted to find you and the Patrol."

"I'm sorry I didn't take you with me when you came to Dandelion. We would have protected each other."

"I knew better, finally they persuaded me how easy," Beti Kacie says. "We were to follow the gray trail."

"Besides, Beti Kacie could fly home if we met trouble," adds Evan Roy.

Rhyonna studies their faces and asks, "Then what happened?"

"Let me tell!" says Princess Lessie Shelly. "We wiped up the dust for a while . . ." Princess Lessie Shelly pauses, looking guilty.

Beti Kacie continues, ". . . off we flew to followed the gray trail through the Meadow of Flowers to the Oak trees"

"The sun was hot. We got tired," says Princess Lessie Shelly.

With irritation Evan Roy adds, "The gray trail disappeared with the heat. We were thirsty and hungry. We rested in the shade of a large Oak tree."

Anxiously Princess Lessie Shelly states, "We were LOST! And scared!"

With worry Evan Roy says, "We heard a rustling. We jumped! Ready to fly."

"We saw a huge spider creeping toward us. We froze!" says Beti Kacie.

Princess Lessie Shelly draws a huge circle with her hands. "A GIANT spider!"

"The giant spider had gray strips on her back and legs, long legs, and a round head with several eyes, black eyes," says Darren Gale.

With disgust Evan Roy agrees, "Ugly spider!"

"UGLY!" sing the four Flyers.

With alarm, Evan Roy says, "We could not fly or yell."

Then the four giggle with smiles spreading over their tale. Quite interested, Rhyonna with Healer Leanna, and Mother Emma wait.

Beti Kacie says, "In a charming voice, the spider said, 'Sweet Faeries . . .'"

" . . . like she wanted to eat us," interrupts Princess Lessie Shelly.

"Yes!" agree the other Flyers.

Darren Gale giggles, "Only, the spider asked, 'Sweet Faeries, do the Seamstresses know you are out here?'"

The four laugh and flutter around Dandelion. Mother Emma and Healer Leanne laugh with the four.

"What happened?" asks Rhyonna annoyed.

Her name is Erwina," says Darren Gale.

"She is an Orb Weaver and works with the Seamstresses Mynra and Varda," says Beti Kacie.

"Spider Erwina saved us," exclaims Princess Lessie Shelly.

The Four Flyers look at each other and nod in agreement.

"Spider Erwina, found you. Thank goodness!"

"We told Spider Erwina we were lost," says Darren Gale. "She encouraged us to sit on her back."

"Among hard, thick hairs," says Beti Kacie.

". . . smelly hairs," grumbles Princess Lessie Shelly.

Evan Roy interrupts, "She took us from orb web to orb web. We met other huge striped spiders."

"Orb Weavers look alike," says Princess Lessie Shelly.

"All her friends work for the Seamstresses. Each spider knew we were coming," Darren Gale says.

The four Flyers become quiet and look at each other, remembering.

Then Beti Kacie tells, "Each spiders offered us bug's juice to drink."

"From dead flies wrapped up," frets Princess Lessie Shelly.

"Icky!" the four say together.

"Some spiders gathered us pollen that was good," Beti Kacie admits.

"Erwina let us walk on the webs. Some webs are sticky." Evan Roy adds.

"Sticky!" repeats Princess Lessie Shelly.

"I lost a shoe!" Evan Roy holds up his foot and still no shoe.

"For days we traveled with Erwina," says Darren Gale.

"One day," corrects Beti Kacie.

"The spiders loved us," says Princess Lessie Shelly.

With regret, Darren Gale adds, "After that great adventure, Erwina took us to Seamstresses Mynra and Varda."

"I was sad to leave Spider Erwina. She is nice," says Princess Lessie Shelly.

With sadness, Beti Kacie, Darren Gale, and Evan Roy agree.

"When we got to the village, we were greeted with love, then told we caused everyone concern and worry, especially our parents," says Darren Gale.

Beti Kacie adds, "Queen Tanya and King Grady are to talk with the Elders."

"What are Queen Tanya and King Grady to do?"

Mother Emma says, "The Elders decided today." She hands to everyone pollen to nibble. Rhyonna slowly chews, enjoying each moment of fun with her Flyers.

Then Healer Leanna gives Rhyonna a piece of raw garlic to eat. Next, Rhyonna chews bitter cherry tree bark. "Take little bites, chew all afternoon. The bark will steady your stomach. Your wings are wrapped; sleep very carefully tonight."

When the warm, friendly sun is high in the sky, Healer Leanna and Mother Emma ready to return to the village.

Not moving, the four Flyers beg, "Let us stay, please." Their arms and legs cling so tightly around the stems of Dandelion that the flowers bend low. Rhyonna knows this trick.

At that moment, floating beside Dandelion is a huge, beastly spider with Seamstresses Mynra and Varda on her back. They glide down a rope of silk and land on Dandelion.

With amazement the four Flyers call, "Erwina!" They flutter to the spider and hug the huge beast as best they can.

Rhyonna greets the orb spider. "Erwina is a friend."

"Yes, Rhyonna, I presented these four wee Faeries to every spider friend I have. We had an adventure."

The four Flyers nod their heads in agreement.

Mother Emma says, "Erwina, glad you are here." Then asks, "Healer Leanna and I must leave to attend the BlackBerry bushes. May these four Flyers ride back to the village on you?"

"I will be happy to carry these four back."

Seamstress Mynra offers, "We will fly back with Erwina, also."

The four Flyers eagerly flutter, flip, tumble, and pop in the air. Then, willingly, they sit on top of Erwina, who purrs in a spider's way. Rhyonna admires how the huge Orb Weaver gained the trust of the Tawnyee Flyers.

Healer Leanna says, "Rhyonna, your mother and I will return in the early morning." After many hugs Mother Emma and Healer Leanna fly towards the village.

Seamstress Mynra turns to Rhyonna. "We told Erwina your story of Zzuf, the horrid fluff, the Grayed Ladybugs, and the ants that helped you."

"Rhyonna, my family and friends want to help in any way we can."

Lacking the words to say how pleased this makes her, Rhyonna nods to Erwina. "You will know when."

Before Rhyonna recovers from Erwina's generous offer, the Seamstresses hold up a dress. In the light the silk sparkles. This gift causes tears to gather in Rhyonna's eyes. The Tawnyee Flyers flutter to comfort Rhyonna, who sobs, "Everyone is so helpful."

Seamstress Varda emphasizes, "With Erwina's fine silk, we wove this dress for you. The yellow comes from the mustard flowers."

"Yellow is my favorite color. Thank you. Erwina, Mynra, and Varda, what can I give you for the dress?"

Seamstress Mynra replies, "Rhyonna, you have already given to us, by returning home."

"And you have Zzuf to rid from ours and others. That is your special thanks."

The Seamstresses remove the tattered rags from Rhyonna, taking special care with her wings. Then they help Rhyonna into the clean silk dress.

"When we wove the dress, we considered your bandaged wings and put ties up the back."

"Thank you." Rhyonna smooths the silk with her hands. "The dress fits, so comfortable, so soft."

Rhyonna hugs Seamstresses Mynra and Varda and gives her best hug to Spider Erwina.

The Tawnyee Flyers climb on the back of Erwina ready for the trip back to the village. Just as Erwina readies to jump on her web string, Queen Tanya and King Grady fly toward Dandelion.

Four Flyers disappear from the top of Erwina and hide in Dandelion. They peek through the leaves. Rhyonna calls them, "Tawnyee Flyers, come here and curtsey to your Queen and King."

Queen Tanya speaks, "No need to be formal. We come with a good message. The Elders have considered Rhyonna's flying adventure and that of the Tawnyee Flyers."

King Grady stands next to the Queen adding, "Lessons were learned by all in these adventures, that is Teacher Rhyonna and the Tawnyee Flyers: Beti Kacie, Evan Roy, Princess Lessie Shelly, and Darren Gale. And after they acknowledge communication with parents is most important, We, Queen Tanya, myself, with the Elders, decree that Flying Lessons can continue."

Before any Flyer can flutter around, Queen Tanya directs, "All stand still."

With the help of the four Flyers, Rhyonna stands leaning on them.

"With Spider Edwina, Seamstresses Mynra and Varda as witness, repeat after me," Queen Tanya says, "We, Teacher Rhyonna, Princess Lessie Shelly, Evan Roy, Beti Kacie, and Darren Gale, will forevermore inform our parents or the King and Queen before leaving BlackBerry Village to venture anywhere at any time. We are responsible members of the village."

Queen Tanya touches Rhyonna's head. "Brawny Rhyonna Faery remains the Flying Teacher for the Wee Flyers, which includes the four Tawnyee Flyers."

Rhyonna curtseys and the four Flyers flutter to steady her. Then the four Flyers curtsey and hug Queen Tanya and King Grady.

Mynra and Varda with Erwina applaud. The four Flyers jump around shouting, "Flying lessons!" Rhyonna throws winning smiles to the four Tawnyee Flyers, who smile back.

Queen Tanya suggests, "Rhyonna, start easy as you gain strength and your wings heal. Start with the Tawnyee Flyers, when feeling stronger, continue your lessons with the Wee Ones."

Rhyonna glows brightly, her greatest worry over. "I'm still the Flying Teacher."

Looking at the four Flyers Rhyonna says, "Tomorrow we start, when the sun is up."

The four Flyers jump, dipping, diving, and spiraling around Dandelion.

Then huge Erwina hugs the four Flyers and turns to Rhyonna, *"I'll come back tomorrow. Remember the offer from the spiders to help with Zzuf."*

Erwina disappears into the trees.

After many thrown kisses, the Tawnyee Flyers with Seamstresses Mynra and Varda, Queen Tanya, and King Grady flutter back to the village.

Assured that two worries are over, the safety of the four Flyers and her flying lessons, Rhyonna relaxes. Sitting alone in the comfort of Dandelion, her thoughts wander to Keegan, Caddee, and Prince Blaire. With all her energy, Rhyonna thrusts a message to her Friends. "I'm home, Keegan. I miss you. Caddee, talk to me. Prince Blaire, you are needed. Come home."

Only scattered feelings return. After long moments of concern, Rhyonna sinks into fears for her Friends, who might be captives of the horrid Zzuf.

Rhyonna comforts herself with a loud shout. "I am healing. I will fly again. Zzuf will be cleansed from ours, and the others. I will do this."

The others listening sing courage to Rhyonna.

Rhyonna leans into Dandelion. The evening shadow signals Dandelion to wrap her petals. Rhyonna rests for tomorrow's flying lesson with the Tawnyee Flyers.

14 - FRIENDS RETURN

AS DANDELION OPENS, sunshine sparkles and flashes into Rhyonna's eyes. Blinking, then blinking again, Rhyonna sees Keegan, Caddee, and Prince Blaire flying to Dandelion. As the three Friends approach, their shouts stream to Rhyonna. The shouts become louder, "RHYONNA! YOU'RE HOME!"

Astounded, Rhyonna stands to greet her returning Friends. They fly, somewhat exhausted and scuffed. No fluff is on them. Rhyonna's joyous "Hello!" drowns in their excitement.

Keegan flies straight to Rhyonna and greets her with a warm embrace and long, most tender hug. Rhyonna hugs Keegan back. Caddee and then Prince Blaire hug Rhyonna. The joy of seeing her Friends sends Rhyonna spinning and sitting on Dandelion.

Quietly Rhyonna speaks. "I must be careful. I am healing."

Surprised, the three Friends settle on the flower with Rhyonna observing her wings. Nothing is spoken about the spider webbing protecting them or the dark soured patches on her skin.

A thick silence hovers around Dandelion. Rhyonna needs to break their sorrow. They are safe, and that is the most important.

Rhyonna speaks. "The horrid parasitic fluff did this. My mistake."

Fear about her wings show on her Friends' faces and in their eyes. With brave confidence Rhyonna offers, "My wings heal. I will fly again!"

Caddee, in her most supportive way, responds, "We know you will."

Promise shines in her Friends' eyes. The concerns about Rhyonna's wings stay unspoken for now. They cuddle Rhyonna for a long while and ask no questions.

Finally, Rhyonna asks, "Where have you been?"

In his cheering joking tone, Keegan replies, "Looking for you, of course."

Rhyonna laughs with the relief.

Then loud, intense shouts from the villagers ring through the meadow to Dandelion. Hugs and tears go round and around. Families are pleased the three friends are as safe as Rhyonna. After much love from the adults, Rhyonna's Friends with the Tawnyee Flyers settle on Dandelion. The villagers and families sit on flowers in the Meadow to hear the adventure. Rhyonna is ready.

Keegan starts the story for all to listen.

"After the Junior Patrol returned, we were told that Rhyonna followed the gray trail and had not returned. Most alarmed, with Prince Blaire and Caddee, we flew to our secret place by the creek. When we heard Rhyonna's calls for help, we decided to fly to Oakee, and ask the Sheegahshee in the old Oak tree. That's where the gray trail ended."

"The fluff was gone," Caddee adds, "dried into thin ropes entangling the flowers like spider webs. By Oakee grew a patch of the strange fluff, maybe a mold of a kind we had never seen before. It smothered the arum plant."

Prince Blaire says, "We knew the arum flower was Rhyonna's favorite bath."

"That's where I was captured. Did any of you touch the fluffy hair sticking out from the arum?"

Keegan and Caddee look at Prince Blaire. Rhyonna studies him. There seem to be no sours on his skin or wings.

"We saw a battle," Keegan continues. "We followed the path of a dragged flower; then the path stopped. The wilted flower was covered with dead fluff. We thought, what if Rhyonna . . . "

A long pause waits until Rhyonna says, "That's werc I was dragged into dumbing goop."

"We had no idea where to look," Caddee says. "No trail to follow, gone. We flew back to Oakee."

"Old Sheegahshee Oakee offered, 'Brawny Faery Rhyonna flew into that arum's flower and did not come out. Some fluffy gray creatures dragged the flower with Faery Rhyonna inside. I could hear her screams for help,'" tells Prince Blaire.

"We decided to climb the hill where the caves were to find an entrance," says Keegan. The thistles were unbearable. We were exhausted from the day of flying. As the dark of evening settled around us, we ate thistle pollen, and Prince Blaire made us soft thistle beds."

"We heard Rhyonna's voice, muffled, like drowning," Prince Blaire says. "We tried to call home and only noise came back."

"In the dark with no fire, we were very anxious," Caddee adds.

"We could not sleep," adds Keegan. "Too many sounds around the hill, the smell of dying damp thistles agitating and causing us to sneeze and our eyes to itch, then night creatures talk."

"A moth hiding somewhere under the thistles flew out at us," continues Prince Blaire. "So we got up and hiked up the hill."

"The thistles were too thick for walking," Keegan says. "So we flew over them. We found the top of the hill."

With a scary voice Prince Blaire says, "A flash of light poked through the thistles, and . . . and . . . A GIGANTIC ANT . . ." Prince Blaire lunges, ". . . LEAPED at us!"

Rhyonna and everyone jump.

"I was ready to . . . run," says Caddee.

"I thought the ants had Rhyonna." Keegan expands, "I was angered, ready to fight. Only, the giant guard ant asked, 'Faeries from the BlackBerry bushes, is Faery Rhyonna home? Queen Floree worries.'"

Caddee adds, "An ant asking about a faery's safety?"

"That was Guard Prior; she helped me."

Prince Blaire continues, "The guard explained when Faery Rhyonna climbed out of the colony, she helped the Faery to the lake. Later, when she checked the Faery was gone.'"

With great concern Caddee says, "That's when the guard told us about the fluff in the caves. And that Rhyonna's wings had the strange fluff on them."

A silent stills the accounting while all look at Rhyonna's wings.

When the sadness clears, Prince Blaire explains, "We wanted to know where the caves were and we wanted to see the fluff. Just then, four small ants appeared, happy to see us, and saying they helped Faery Rhyonna climb out of the colony."

"Those are the Scouts I caught in the cave eating in the fluff."

"We followed the four Scouts down to the lake. They showed us a cave entrance. We wanted to go inside," Keegan says.

"They blocked our way," Caddee adds.

"Zzuf, the horror, lives there."

Prince Blaire continues, "Just at that time, Dragonfly Majestic whizzed by, then whizzed back. He landed, saying that Rhyonna is back on her Dandelion."

"Yes, I asked Majestic to watch for you."

Keegan expands, "Majestic said, 'I took Rhyonna to the village. I fear she will never fly.'"

Rhyonna interrupts for all to hear. "I will fly!"

A warm breeze tosses *"I will fly!"* into the leaves of the trees, which also whisper, *"Fly! Fly! I will!"* Rhyonna's affirm repeats over and over. With silent accord, villagers, animals, and the others identify with Rhyonna's determination.

After the healing quiets, Caddee returns to the adventure. "The four ants hurried us to the

Meadow of Flowers where they said Faery Rhyonna sits on her Dandelion."

"Are the Scout here?"

"No, the four went back to the colony," replies Prince Blaire. "They said, 'Tell Rhyonna the ants are well. Our Queen Floree will forever thank Brawny Faery Rhyonna. Remember we are ready to help.'"

Regarding the villagers, Rhyonna hopes for a turn of heart for the ants. Faces do show sadness and concern.

At this time, Healer Leanna and Mother Emma fly to Rhyonna. Healer Leanna says, "Facing that monster, not yet. You are still healing."

Queen Tanya steps forward. "King Grady and I declare a celebration for our dearest sons and daughters and their safe return. In four days from now. This will give us time to prepare foods and drinks and invite others who want to come."

The villagers give a forceful, lively cheer. Rhyonna watches them fly happily back to the village because, besides the continuous cleaning up, a festival is on the way.

All the Flyers hug and hug Rhyonna until Mother Emma says, "Enough, go catch the villagers. Remember, watch, and protect." Weary Keegan, Caddee, and Prince Blaire leave after many thrown kisses.

Healer Leanna removes the web bandages. Again, she creams the pains and anxiety for Rhyonna. "The sours are gone; only light yellow spots show in the gossamer green. In time, the small holes will mend together, allowing you to fly."

Twisting, Rhyonna tries to see the spots. "I'll be the only one with spotted wings. How ugly is that?" Discouragement rushes at Rhyonna. "I'll never fly. Only in my dreams."

"Rhyonna," comforts Healer Leanna, "the yellow of the spots matches your dress."

"Dearest Daughter, the spots tell of the adventure you survived. They are you, showing your strength and courage. You will be the best Flyer in the village. You will fly again."

Rhyonna encouraged says, "And, I will rid that horrid Zzuf from our realms."

Healer Leanna cuddles Rhyonna. "For now, go slow, think wisely, and ask for help. You can walk, or your friends can carry you. Just watch your wings. Move them occasionally to build your muscles. I'll see you in the evening."

Mother Emma embraces Rhyonna, "We are very proud of you."

As the sun settles on the day slipping behind the Oaks, Rhyonna stands on a fresh flower of Dandelion, soaking in the evening colors while gently moving her wings back and forth. Rhyonna munches Dandelion's pollen.

With resolve Rhyonna sings:

My Dandelion, thanks for giving to me.
I eat your crunchy pollen.
I love the tart, zestful taste.
I have your power, strength, and courage.
My Dandelion. I will fly.

15 - FAERY FUN

IN THE LATE MORNING while the sun stands on top of the Oak trees, Rhyonna crunches leisurely on Dandelion's pollen, observing Mizzee Bee. Fast and with purpose, she gathers Dandelion's pollen. Rhyonna has a purpose to defeat Zzuf.

Keegan whistles from the distant shadows among the trees. Rhyonna glimpses her Friends escorting four Tawnyee Flyers to Dandelion. Happy and excited, the Flyers soar to Dandelion. Natural, easily done with little effort, each flies; with practice Rhyonna will fly.

Keegan rushes to Rhyonna and gives her a gentle kiss on her cheek. The four Flyers giggle and flutter around. After long hardy hugs and "good morning" greetings, the four Flyers with Keegan, Caddee, and Prince Blaire settle on Dandelion's flowers.

"This morning," Caddee reports to Rhyonna, "we were called to stand with our families before the Elders, Queen Tanya, and King Grady because we left the village without telling anyone. We were afraid we lost our status. No more teaching and no more Junior Patrol."

"After much discussion and many questions," expands Keegan, "the Elders decided our intentions were good. Only next time, we need to communicate with our parents as well as the Queen and King whenever going beyond the boundaries of the Meadow of Flowers."

"We heard how worried our parents were, each one spoke to us," Caddee says.

Prince Blaire adds, "We agreed and told the Elders, from now on before we go on another rescue or anywhere, we will inform the Queen where and why. When we arrive where we are going, we send a message to the Queen."

"Queen Tanya will keep the village informed about us," Caddee adds.

Keegan offers, "We understand why the Elders and our families need to trust us."

"Prince Blaire was brave and direct. The Elders were pleased with his replies," Keegan adds.

"I will always tell my Mother Emma and the Queen when I leave. We are privileged to live on our flowers outside the village."

Caddee adds, "We must tell each other when we leave and take a friend with us. That includes the Tawnyee Flyers who are ready for more responsibility."

The Flyers listen with ears and eyes wide.

"We will all take an oath, 'The Communication Oath,'" suggests Prince Blaire. "We are responsible to others, to ourselves, and to our families with absolute trust from now on and forevermore."

With her Friends, Rhyonna and four Flyers nod their heads in agreement, pausing with silent understanding. Hands stack on top of hands and slowly rise up and down, binding Friends and words.

Despair catches Rhyonna. "This oath bounds me to be safe. All this confusion caused by my carelessness." Immediately Rhyonna's regrets and dread expand to touch all others who hear.

The four Flyers fly to and cuddle Rhyonna. No Friend speaks. Caddee hugs Rhyonna. Dandelion nestles her. The flowers, trees, the animals, insects, birds, and the others in between stop their chatter to respect Rhyonna.

"Rhyonna, to blame yourself is wrong. We all learned. Many times, you flew to the arum flower without any danger," Caddee offers.

"Without your adventure, we would never know what the horrid Zzuf desires," Prince Blaire reassures.

"Remember your success, escaping from Zzuf to warn all of us, all that courage," Keegan adds.

"I did find that horrid parasite. I did escape. Zzuf must be destroyed, right now, before the worst happens to us and the others."

"Rhyonna, we need that strength," Prince Blaire says.

The four Flyers sit quietly next to Rhyonna, listening. Noticing the four Flyers, Caddee says, "Today the Tawnyee Flyers are here to have fun, to ease your distress." Rhyonna gives them a special, loving hug.

Keegan whistles and points. Far away in the distance, a dot jumps, soars up into the air, falls down into the flowers, and jumps again. The dot turns toward the whistle and Dandelion.

"I know that is a grasshopper," declares Evan Roy.

"Captain Keegan's familiar?" asks Princess Lessie Shelly.

Prince Blaire remarks, "Yes, of course, love of danger and thrill."

"My grasshopper is called McFargan."

The four Flyers laugh and repeat, "Mc FAR gone!"

"Who is ready to ride Mc FAR gone?"

Grasshopper McFargan hops onto Dandelion beside Rhyonna. He readies to nibble a leaf. Keegan corrects his friend, "Never eat this Dandelion. This is Rhyonna's flower."

The grasshopper bows in a grasshopper's way to Rhyonna.

Rhyonna understands. "Grasshoppers are always hungry."

"Ready for a ride, Flyers?"

The four flutter up and perch on the back of the grasshopper. Keegan balances near McFargan's head, grabbing his feelers. "Hang on, Flyers! Okay McFargan, give us your best ride."

Rhyonna, with Teacher Caddee and Prince Blaire watch the grasshopper's powerful back legs push down while the front legs rise up, then the back legs spring. McFargan leaps into the air. Four mouths open and screams of pleasure ring. McFargan flips out his wings, which buzz and drown their shouts. Then down onto leaves of grass McFargan falls. The four Flyers hold tight to McFargan with their legs while arms bond around each other, bumping up and down.

Rhyonna laughs and Caddee and Prince Blaire join her.

Keegan asks, "More?"

Shouts of "YES" chime.

McFargan jumps for a second round. Two other grasshoppers join him, buzzing.

When McFargan lands, the four Flyers leap off and jump onto flowers. Other grasshoppers join McFargan, bouncing here and there. Energized and invigorated, Keegan jumps from flower to flower then dashes back to Dandelion, laughing.

Prince Blaire grumbles, "The bees are upset."

Princess Lessie Shelly tells, "A bee is my brother's familiar."

"The Queen! I like the busy working bees and they happily sing all the time, except when preening. I asked a bee to be my familiar and she said, 'I live such a short life, I will ask Queen.' The bee did a dance with another bee and asked me to fly with them."

The four Flyers gather closer to Prince Blaire. He straightens his crown. "I entered the hive and was shown the wax making, the honey making, the special foods given to the babies, and then taken to the Queen, called Mizzee Queen."

Rhyonna chuckles with the four Flyers.

"That's right, Mizzee Queen. FUNNY! I did not laugh. She was pleased a Prince from the Faery village wanted a worker bee as a familiar; she said she was impressed by my gracious manners."

Everyone listening chuckles while the wind dances the laughter around. Rhyonna is happy.

Prince Blaire looks around, pleased. "She said that although I was a male she would be my familiar, because male Faeries need to work. And the villagers allowed her workers to take pollen from the BlackBerry flowers."

Beti Kacie asks, "Do you fly on the Mizzee Queen?"

"Oh, no, she is too busy laying the eggs. I have permission to fly on any bee. I know the dance to ask."

The four Flyers look at Rhyonna, then at their Prince, then at the bees flying.

"Oh, you want to fly on a worker?"

Rhyonna answered for them and herself. "Of course we do."

Prince Blaire leaps into the air and dances with a bee. That bee dances with another until eight bees buzz to Dandelion.

"Fly onto their backs, quickly and gently."

Rhyonna waits on the Dandelion. Prince Blaire flies a dance to a bee, which dashes over to Rhyonna and calmly lands.

"*Fazzeeeeerzzz!*" Mizzee buzzes.

Rhyonna bows. "Mizzee Bee."

Keegan and Caddee help Rhyonna onto the back of Mizzee Bee.

Prince Blaire directs, "Hold onto the feelers, so you can lead the bee."

The bees buzz around the meadow and enter flowers here and there, collecting pollens. Rhyonna is astonished by Mizzee's steady even flight and with the hum of buzzing coming from her wings

Mizzee Bee buzzes, *"Zzeeengg ZZZonggg."*

Laughing, Rhyonna understands Mizzee's joke.

All too soon, Prince Blaire with his bee does a dance. All the bees return to Dandelion; the Faeries slide off. With her Friends, Rhyonna and the Tawnyee Flyers take the pollens offered by the bees.

Rhyonna thanks the bees, patting Mizzee Bee.

"Your ride was wonderful, so rich, so fast. I will fly like that."

"zYozz zwillzz," sing the bees as they fly to their work.

With admiration, Rhyonna smiles at Prince Blaire. "I always wanted to fly on a bee, only thought they were too busy working."

16 - FAERY POND

WITH HER PARTY OF FRIENDS, Rhyonna and the Tawnyee Flyers relax on Dandelion eating sweet pollens the bees offered. Hummingbirds play in the air, darting here, then there. One hummingbird darts by, stops, and swoops to Dandelion and flitters back and forth, observing.

The hummingbird glimpses at Rhyonna, then observes each Tawnyee Flyer. "*I Hue. Fly, one to my nest?*"

Evan Roy stands up, ready. "Rhyonna, may I visit his nest?"

"Yes. Be prepared to tell us what you see. We will be at the creek by the small pond."

Keegan adds, "Their nests are hidden. None of us have seen a hummingbird nest. You are lucky, Evan Roy."

Hummingbird Hue stares at Keegan while Evan Roy steadies on his back. Rhyonna notices the intense look.

"I'll meet you at the small pond," says Evan Roy. With a whirr, Hummingbird Hue dashes out of sight in a blur.

Prince Blaire chides, "Hue is not sure of you, Keegan. Looking for nests?"

Rhyonna smiles at Caddee, "Time to show these Flyers your familiar. They will never guess."

Darren Gale, Beti Kacie, and Princess Lessie Shelly concentrate, calculating who might be Caddee's familiar.

Caddee smiles. "We need to fly to the creek. I mean walk to the creek for Rhyonna. On the way, you can guess who my familiar is."

Keegan and Prince Blaire bend Rhyonna's flower and Caddee helps her slide to the ground. Rhyonna leans on Keegan and Prince Blaire. With the party, Rhyonna walks slowly through the grasses and flowers. The hot ground sweats earth odors, which slows Rhyonna's progress; the party waits for her. In the path is a small brown snail.

Princess Lessie Shelly guesses, "I know that snail, the one crawling over there."

Caddee walks to the snail and pats its shell. "Slime, can Rhyonna ride on your back?"

The three Flyers help Rhyonna up onto his shell. Slowly the snail moves toward the creek with Rhyonna. The snail goes slower and slower.

"Slime looks tired. He needs to travel by himself," Caddee says.

"Slime, that was safe," thanks Rhyonna. He pulls his eyes and body into his shell, exhausted.

"Slime is asleep," Keegan says.

The three Flyers giggle. Then they jump and flutter about the flowers. Rhyonna loves their fun.

Princess Lessie Shelly guesses, "I know, that roly-poly over there."

Caddee pats the roly-poly, who rolls into a ball. "I do like the way she protects herself."

Keegan offers, "The ride would be like balancing on a round stone with ribs carved on it."

The three Flyers giggle. Rhyonna chuckles with their delight.

Just then, from under the bending grass, crawls a black moth. His large black eyes shine. The three

Flyers scream. Captain Keegan and Prince Blaire draw their daggers then laugh.

"Just a moth named Sweet," says Caddee.

The moth shakes its wings, stops, and stares. His feelers wiggle and he crawls toward Caddee.

Darren Gale chuckles, "Must be Moth Sweet?"

Rhyonna likes this game; the Flyers can observe the others before choosing their familiars.

Caddee shakes her head 'no' while she pats the moth. "Once I found his hiding place, like today, and we became friends. He lets me ride on him, only he flies at night." The moth crawls back under the blades of grass

Turning Rhyonna stops, frozen, and stares into long harden gray strings tangled in a mound. The four Flyers and her Friends gasp; the others in the meadow stop singing.

Captain Keegan says, "Looks like the long gray strings under the Oak tree, where we . . ." Keegan hesitates.

"An hornet caught," Prince Blaire adds.

"That could be me," Rhyonna sobs.

Caddee cuddles Rhyonna.

No sounds stir in the meadow. For a long while all absorb into Rhyonna's fears. Finally Rhyonna speaks, "No, that is not me. Zzuf will dry up."

Relief twirls around, the others in the meadow move and sing with confidence.

During the remaining walk to the creek, three Flyers play touch-tag, jumping from flower to flower. Playfully, the three flutter here and there with Captain Keegan and Prince Blaire chasing.

Rhyonna laughs with the fun.

A toad pops his head out of the sand in their path. The three Flyers scatter and hide behind flowers. Caddee flies to the old toad and strokes his bumpy head. "This is Old Gruff."

The three Flyers pat him. Old Gruff pulls himself out of the sand and hops to Rhyonna. *"Welcome dear Faery. I feared you lost."*

"Did Caddee tell you, Old Gruff?"

"My first time to see Caddee in a long while. Ants carry seeds and the latest gossip. Though, have not seen ants in a long while."

Beti Kacie guesses, "Caddee, Old Gruff is your familiar?"

Old Gruff puffs one of his grunts, his laugh; that makes the three Flyers giggle.

"No, Old Gruff is the familiar of a witch, not a faery," Caddee says.

"Right, a witch."

Old Gruff digs into the sand.

"More later, sand is protection from fluff."

"We will linger until you are completely covered." Slowly as possible, he digs into the nice warm sand until buried. The three Flyers marvel at his disappearance. They flutter back and forth over Old Gruff's hiding spot.

Keegan remarks, "The ants scare, Old Gruff."

At that instance, Majestic whizzes above Rhyonna. He pops and lands on a branch of a willow by the pond. Tucking in his wings, he faces the party. *"At the pond to watch the nymphs eat mosquito larvae and pupae."*

Darren Gale, Princess Lessie Shelly, and Beti Kacie stare, calculating the size and grandeur of the giant facing them.

Rhyonna smiles at the Flyers, "Why I am the best flyer in the Village, racing Majestic."

"Yes, my service to Faery Rhyonna, good player."

Princess Lessie Shelly asks, "Rhyonna, how do I choose a Dragonfly?"

"Majestic, Lessie Shelly is interested, she needs a champion, as her familiar."

"I'm glad to say, Princess. Pick a nymph and think about flying with the Dragonfly."

Beti Kacie asks, "Please, can I have a Dragonfly?"

"Yes, all the Tawnyee Flyers can ask for a Dragonfly."

Majestic rotates around the branch. *"Give the nymph a name. Call the name often. The nymph will dream of you. In three seasons, the nymph becomes a Dragonfly. He or she will search for you."*

Princess Lessie Shelly says, "Giant. Yes, Giant will be my Dragonfly's name."

Majestic stands proud. *"Remember each year to choose a nymph. Have your next party about this time."*

"I'll remind everyone," says Princess Lessie Shelly.

"Three years, Princess, then a dragonfly each year."

Prince Blaire offers, "Shall we call Princess Lessie Shelly the Keeper of the Dragonfly Nymphs?"

Rhyonna with Caddee, Keegan, the other two Flyers, and Majestic agree.

Prince Blaire asserts, "I'll suggest the title to my Mother and Father. We have a new title among the Faeries, Keeper of the Dragonfly Nymphs. The First Keeper is Princess Lessie Shelly."

Majestic buzzes his wings and pops into the sky.

Darren Gale looks pleased but left out. Rhyonna reminds him, "There are many more familiars. Think whom you enjoy."

SPLASH! The water jumps! Everyone jumps! Into the pond dives Keegan, and just as fast as he dives in, out Keegan splashes on a large green frog.

"Keegan, just your style, hopping and leaping!"

Caddee rushes to the edge of the pool. "Keegan, the careful, the water skippers."

Darren Gale, Beti Kacie, and Princess Lessie Shelly sing, "Water skipper!"

Caddee nods, "Want to ride on one?" She leads the party to the edge of the water, bends down, and gently taps to make ripples. A water skipper skates over. "This is my familiar, Skippy."

The three Flyers giggle, "Skippy."

Prince Blaire stares at Caddee. "Why a water skipper?"

"I was here one day looking for my minnow, watching the water skippers having a good time. I flew up and gently landed on the back of Skippy. He went on skipping over the water and his family danced around us. The next time I came to the pool, Skippy skated over to me."

Beti Kacie asks, "So fly to a water skipper and gently land on their back and ride?"

"Yes, keep your wings arched ready to fly, in case you start to fall. Softly use your wings to lift off the skipper. They will sink into the water if you jump."

Rhyonna cherishes the fun and these moments with her Flyers and Friends and all the others in the Meadow. The play is so reviving, so real. Their concerns for her are appreciated.

As the Flyers ride the skippers, one long silk thread dangles to the water, then another and another. Rhyonna looks up. Spider Erwina lets silk strings fall from a willow tree. "Erwina, what are you doing?"

I'm spinning a rope.

Darren Gale flies up and pats the huge spider. He slides down the silk strings, squeezing them together.

"Rhyonna, take hold of the silk rope and slide across the water."

With help from Keegan, Rhyonna holds the web rope and balances on the water. Gently Keegan pushes. Wiggling but balanced by her wings, Rhyonna slides to the opposite bank of the creek.

"WHEEEEeeee! That is fun."

Everyone takes turns sliding back and forth across the creek. Water sprays from the pond, creating a humor of sparkles mixed with laughter. Rhyonna loves her friends.

"What a great idea, Erwina,"

"The silk rope will stay here, I've woven it around the branch over the creek. Come web slide any time."

Spider Erwina turns to Rhyonna. *"Remember, the spiders want to help purge the fluff."*

The help from the spiders Rhyonna welcomes. Only words of gratefulness are lost in the pressing burden of Rhyonna's doubts.

"Erwina, I need to heal my wings and fly."

"The longer you wait, Rhyonna, the more this horror eats into the others."

"Rhyonna, when you are ready," Caddee consoles. The faces of her Friends and the Flyers offer reassurance.

"Erwina, tell the spiders soon, real soon."

Prince Blaire breaks the heaviness. "Cheer for Darren Gale, the First Keeper of the Orb Spiders and Their Webs. I will suggest, no, tell, Mom and Dad about this new title."

Spider Erwina gives Darren Gale a spider hug. *"I must be off to tend my webs."* The other Flyers pat Spider Erwina. *"Rhyonna, at the ant colony by the gray caves, sooner than soon."*

Shouts from Evan Roy are heard. "We are back!" Hummingbird Hue flies to the pond. Evan Roy slides off. While Hue drinks water, Rhyonna notes how Evan Roy strokes the hummingbird with much affection.

"Hue's nest is deep inside the tangles of the BlackBerry bushes close to the village. Hue wonders about the gray fluff on leaves. I told him about the parasite, Zzuf."

Hummingbird Hue twists his head and his tail this way and that, then peers deep into Rhyonna. *"We drink nectars from the BlackBerry flowers. Will fluff grow on us?"*

"No, my Friends and I are to destroy the horror. We will work with the orb spiders and ants from the hill by the lake."

Keegan gently pats Hummingbird Hue. "Think of this danger gone."

"I hear, gone is the fluff."

Prince Blaire offers, "Evan Roy is to be the First Keeper of the Hummingbirds and the Secret of Their Nests. I will tell the Queen and King."

Hue rubs against Evan Roy, who hugs the hummingbird.

"I fly back to my wife and soon-to-be family."

With a hop, wings zipping, Hummingbird Hue departs into the sky and in a blur disappears.

17 - FLOWERS

WITH HER PARTY OF FRIENDS, Rhyonna walks from the peaceful bubbling sounds of the creek through the fragrant Meadow of Flowers, spiced by the warmth of the sun.

At Rhyonna's favorite rock, Keegan cups his hands so Rhyonna can step into them. He gives a push and up Rhyonna goes; Keegan is strong. Up he dashes to the top of the rock; Keegan is fast. Rhyonna takes his hands to pull up.

When the rest of the party flutters to the top of the rock, Lender the Lizard slides away. Rhyonna suggests, "Become quiet and Lender will return and sing with us. He is a dreamer."

Slowly, cautiously, Lender the Lizard crawls from his hole in the rock observing each Faery, while the Faeries sit quietly watching him settle by Rhyonna.

"When does Lender sing?" Darren Gale whispers.

"His song is silent. You will hear it in your mind. Listen."

For a while, Rhyonna with everyone sings a silent song and warms in the sun. All too soon, something alerts Lender and he slides off the rock, waking everyone. Floating in the breeze flutter four zestful butterflies.

Rufus flutters to Rhyonna, *"Finding you, Dear Faeries. Coming for friend for chrysalis."*

The butterflies land on flowers around the rock. Rhyonna with everyone observes the butterflies' landing. Beti Kacie looks at Rhyonna, then shouts, "I'm the one, Keeper of Butterflies."

"Accepting! Befriending! Protecting us."

"How will I know when to find you, Rufus?" Beti Kacie asks.

"Finding eggs, not me. Watching caterpillars eating. Tending their change. Be with chrysalis. Watching their flying."

"Rhyonna, will you help me?" asks Beti Kacie.

"All the Flyers will help in early spring when the flowers grow."

Princess Lessie Shelly, Evan Roy, and Darren Gale nod their heads yes! They move closer to Rufus, admiring his scaled wings.

"Of course, Teacher Caddee, Captain Keegan, and Prince Blaire are invited to come," offers Beti Kacie.

"That will be the best. We will have more parties in the flowers," promises Rhyonna.

Rufus raises his wings and shuffles his feet.

"Protecting then. Playing now, Beti Kacie? Riding, Flyers?"

Beti Kacie gleams. "Dancing in the flowers with Rufuses the Butterflies, now?"

"A friends dance!" Rhyonna suggests. "Some of us dance on the ground and the others dance with the four Rufuses."

Rhyonna with the Flyers and Caddee sit on sorrel flowers while Keegan and Prince Blaire search for the open circle where faeries can dance. "We found a Faery Circle, right over here." Keegan shouts.

The whole party travels to a circle among the daisies. The Rufuses land in the center, holding their wings slightly open and up.

"Dancing, shining warmth. Embracing uplifting."

Four Flyers crawl onto the backs of the butterflies.

"Energizing fun. Fluttering. Floating. Spinning. Enchanting," sings Rufus with his friends as they fly.

The wind blows the sweet song among the flowers harmonizing with the flutter of the butterfly wings. The grasses giggle sweet tones as they bounce rhythms here and there.

Glowing along with Keegan, Caddee, and Prince Blaire, Rhyonna's feet dance. Around and around in the circle, her feet play on the comforting, soft earth.

Singing, her voice is clear and lyrical, singing as everyone twirls, spins, and leaps. Rhyonna forgets her hurt and regrets about the damage to her wings. As Rhyonna dances, her joy and the fun become hardened pieces of light that drop on the earth.

All too soon, the butterflies land the four Flyers inside the circle.

"Flying finishing. Dancing tomorrow?"

Beti Kacie looks at Rhyonna for approval.

"Yes, after all is right and well, we meet the Rufuses after we defeat Zzuf."

Alight with merriment, the four Rufuses flutter on their way.

Prince Blaire is the first to speak. "The First Keeper of the Butterfly Eggs, Caterpillars, and Chrysalis will be Beti Kacie, who now has her special title and job."

Beti Kacie beams at Rhyonna, then flutters, swirls, and spins happily around everyone. Rhyonna respects how proud Beti Kacie is; she makes a huge commitment. All the Flyers have their familiars, a great responsibility for mature Flyers.

"I'll describe these new titles of the Tawnyee Flyers to the Queen and King." There are muffled chuckles. Prince Blaire bows to everyone. Then everyone laughs and bows to their Prince.

Keegan says, "Making decisions, our king-to-be takes his role of title-creating seriously."

Rhyonna with Caddee and the four Flyers smile approval at their Prince.

"Someday, Prince Blaire," says Rhyonna, "you will be our King, and you will be strong."

Prince Blaire lowers his head in his shy way.

While her Friends gather pollens, Rhyonna notes her Friends are as busy as bees. Pensively chewing the refreshment, Rhyonna nestles among the flowers with the four Flyers. Although pleased with the fun, Rhyonna worries about her task with the horrid Zzuf.

"Rhyonna, are you tired?" Caddee asks.

Rhyonna changes the concern, "Has anyone noticed, not one Ladybug anywhere?"

Keegan remarks, "And the sap-suckers stacked thick and sticky."

"No ants, either," Prince Blaire says.

The party with Rhyonna becomes absorbed in the others around them, looking, observing the ground and flowers. Again, Rhyonna considers the fatal risks for her Friends and the others who help rid Zzuf from their realm.

While Rhyonna gathers words to cover her anxiety about the impossibility ahead, Beti Kacie asks, "Do Prince Blaire, Captain Keegan, and

Teacher Caddee have favorite flowers, as Rhyonna has Dandelion?"

"Do any of you know what flower our Prince has?" Taunts Keegan.

"Iris for royalty," Darren Gale answers.

Keegan and Prince Blaire shake their heads.

Beti Kacie comments, "Finding the correct flower is impossible; there are so many flowers with tasty pollens."

"To make this easier, no harsh odor or scent so we have hundreds of flowers left," Darren Gale says.

"Nothing resentful, angry, or unpleasant," Evan Roy adds.

"Nothing salty or sour, tough, or bitter," Princess Lessie Shelly adds.

"Pollen can be lingering, pleasant, tasting most likely sugary, and full of flavor," Beti Kacie adds.

"That means nothing sharp or piercing, although Captain Keegan and Prince Blaire carry jackknives," Darren Gale adds.

Rhyonna with Keegan, Caddee, and Prince Blaire laugh so heartily they topple into the flowers.

Beti Kacie goes on, "Which means, the most fragrant, sweet-tasting, pleasing, desirable, gratifying, satisfying, to also mention kind, thoughtful, generous, charming, endearing to all senses. That is hundreds of flowers to guess."

"Yes," says Evan Roy. "That is the whole Meadow of Flowers in spring, summer, and fall, while many linger into winter."

Rhyonna laughs so joyfully her tears flow.

"Think about what each of us needs. Rhyonna wants the power and courage of the Dandelion for her flight." Caddee suggests.

"The daisy is Captain Keegan's," shouts Beti Kacie. "He brought the pollen from daisy flowers."

"The buttercup is Teacher Caddee's," shouts Darren Gale. "She brought that pollen."

"So what is Prince Blaire's?" Evan Roy questions.

A shout "Rhyonna?" rings into the air from Healer Leanna.

In a flash, Caddee says, "I'll fly and tell Leanna you are coming."

The four Flyers look at Rhyonna, then at Prince Blaire.

"We will not budge until we know his flower," demands Darren Gale.

Rhyonna sings with Keegan and Prince Blaire, "Thistle!"

"Thistle?" echoes Evan Roy.

"What for?" asks Darren Gale.

"I'll tell you on our way to Dandelion," Prince Blaire says."

Keegan helps Rhyonna stand up. Most of the walking Rhyonna does alone, although her balance is wobbly.

Prince Blaire starts, "The thistle is versatile: food, shelter, protection, can be a weapon, and has peppery tasting pollen. The tassels make good sleeping beds. Only the stickers are a problem." Then Prince Blaire adds, "The thistles are a good meeting place, secret and protected."

At Dandelion, Keegan gives Rhyonna a special hug and kiss on the cheek. He whispers, "I love you."

Rhyonna hugs him back. "I know!"

Rhyonna gathers the four Flyers in a hug. "Next time we meet decide what your flower is."

Then her Friends with the four Flyers wave good-bye as they fly back to the village.

Healer Leanna checks Rhyonna's wings. "You did exercise them today. They're much stronger. Fun with others always speeds healing. The yellow sours have stopped growing. Only a few small holes here and there, and the fibers close the holes. You will fly."

As the sun hides behind the Oak trees, on Dandelion rests Rhyonna, thinking about flying. Right now, better balance is needed, which will be tomorrow's lesson.

Dandelion curls, a warm blanket, surrounding Rhyonna, shielding her from the cool of the night. The songs of the crickets with the fragrance of Dandelion subdue Rhyonna, the luckiest, most fortunate, and happiest of all Faeries.

Rhyonna whispers to Dandelion, "Tomorrow, I decide about Zzuf."

18 - OOPS, OFF AGAIN!

EATING HER MORNING POLLEN, Rhyonna observes Dandelion's cousin, a giant plant with enormous flowers, higher than any flower in the meadow. At last, one of the flowers turned into seeds. The Tawnyee Flyers will climb this dandelion and crawl into a seed palace, the perfect lesson for balancing.

Then over by the bushes and Oaks, Rhyonna sees the four Flyers approaching with Teacher Caddee. Rhyonna observes how grown-up the four are: so brave, so ready, maybe too willing, and excellent at flying.

If something happens to the four while out today, Rhyonna dismisses her negative thought. Teacher Caddee will be here to help.

The four Flyers eagerly flutter with smiles beaming to Rhyonna, so happy for this day, after the fun adventure yesterday, ready for their flying lesson. Today will be extraordinary.

After they settle, Rhyonna points to the tall dandelion. "Our flying lesson today is that giant cousin of Dandelion." The Tawnyee Flyers gasp.

"WOW! Caddee exclaims. "That dandelion grew tall. I'll walk with you to the giant."

Rhyonna walks along with Teacher Caddee while the Flyers play flutter tag in the flowers. Getting closer to the giant, the four Flyers fly up into the sky pondering its height. When arriving at the dandelion, the eager Flyers flutter higher and higher to impress Rhyonna, who chuckles.

Teacher Caddee calls to the eager four, who somersault in the air. "Sit on the leaves of the giant dandelion." Then she says to Rhyonna, "I have a meeting with Mother Greer about the school. I'll pick these eager Flyers up later."

"Anything serious?"

"Only our usual, about what topics to teach."

"Like my flying lesson today on balance."

"Yes, since the four had their adventure with the spiders, we need to rework the Flyers' outings. The Tawnyee Flyers are most grown up."

To the four, Teacher Caddee says, "Remember, Rhyonna is healing, be gentle with her, stay close, and help her climb."

"Really, Caddee, I am much stronger."

"Be practical, Rhyonna."

"Caddee, I learned my lesson!" says Rhyonna. "Look at my wings."

Rhyonna has no time to fuss about flying; the four eager Flyers wiggle off the giant's leaf, ready for their adventure.

Rhyonna points to the rock in the Meadow of Flowers. "We will wait on my favorite rock with Lender the Lizard, silently singing!" Rhyonna and Caddee smile the agreement.

"I'll meet you and the Flyers at the rock about noon." Caddee flutters off over the flowers into the shadows of the bushes and Oak trees to the village.

The four sing, "Good-bye, Teacher Caddee."

Darren Gale and Evan Roy help Rhyonna crawl onto a leaf of the huge dandelion. Princess Lessie Shelly and Beti Kacie fly beside her, just in case. The climbing reminds Rhyonna of the tunnels inside the ant colony with the four Scouts.

Slowly, crawling up leaves, Rhyonna climbs up into the tall dandelion. Then with help from the four Flyers steps onto a flower. Rhyonna steps across one huge flower to the next huge flower.

"I must rest." Rhyonna sits with the four Flyers on the longest and largest flower at the top. They eat a bit of pollen. Rhyonna points to a seed cluster at the very tip-top of the dandelion.

"That is my most favorite place in all of the Meadow. We must be careful when we enter." Four faces question Rhyonna.

With the help of the Flyers, Rhyonna crawls inside and through long seed pillars that make a circular dome. Each long pillar stretches high with feathery lace on top. Rays of light from the sun split the lace into colors.

"I always wonder how the yellow petals turn into tall seeds reaching into the colors of the rainbow."

On the palace pad between the towers, Rhyonna sits with the Flyers to observe the shining colors. Silently they absorb the hypnotic spell. Each lace top is a delicate tapestry like a butterfly's wing, breaking the light into binding colors.

Unexpectedly, the wind sways the long-stemmed palace back and forth in a gently soothing rhythm. Then with a fast jerk, the wind rips the seeds from the palace, blowing Rhyonna with the four Flyers into the sky. The wind is not part of the flying lesson.

"Grab a pillar," Rhyonna yells to her Tawnyee Flyers. "Tighten your hands and legs around the stem. The lace umbrella holds up the seed. Balance the seed using your wings. Float with the wind."

The wind snatches the seeds and tosses them higher into the sky. Rhyonna yells, "Let go of the seeds before you are blown higher. The wind will blow me to the lake. Rush to the village and tell my mother and father. I will be by . . ." Her words drown in the song between the wind and seeds.

The four shout to Rhyonna, "Okay!" They soar towards the village.

Rhyonna whimpers then shouts. "I'll walk to the thistles, the THISTLES!"

The four are too far away. Rhyonna shouts anyway, "Tell Keegan, Caddee, and Prince Blaire in the thistles by the clay cave."

"NOT AT THE ROCK!"

Only birds hear and flutter away, leaving Rhyonna sobbing, floating off toward the lake. In panic, Rhyonna freezes, tightly hanging onto the stem.

Steadily, the umbrellas float into the blue vastness of the sky. The wind exhales slowly and lifts the umbrellas higher. Easily, gently, the seeds lift up. When the wind relaxes its blow, the seeds glide down. Ever so slowly and calmly, the umbrellas drift. Rhyonna relaxes, enjoying the rhythms.

The seeds float over the Oak trees, which surround the lake. The leaves of the trees blend into green. The lake echoes the green, which reflects back into the sky.

Blown higher, the seeds glide. Then a swift blow of the wind jerks the seeds. Rhyonna releases her hold before turning upside down.

"I must fly!" Rhyonna shouts to the air.

Ready for anything, Rhyonna stretches her wings to balance. This effort allows her to float. Rhyonna forces air between her wings by pulling down; her wings squeeze. Only air flows through the tiniest holes that are healing.

Falling, Rhyonna opens her wings to glide to the surface of the lake. Feet first Rhyonna readies to land. On the surface, Rhyonna slides until her feet sink. For a while, her wings float on the surface with her head above the water. Rhyonna pledges, yelling to whatever and whomever hear. "I WILL SURVIVE!"

Battling with her feet to balance, Rhyonna holds her heavy soaked wings open. Moving her arms back and forth, too soon, Rhyonna becomes weak and sinks deeper into the water.

Struggling for breath, Rhyonna pulls her wings together to push the water, only not enough to lift her. Taking her last breath, Rhyonna sinks deeper into the cold water. Her thought is SURVIVE.

Onto the back of Fish, Rhyonna slides. GRABBING! Aware Fish is here, Rhyonna's legs and arms hug the power. To the surface of the water, Fish pushes Rhyonna, who gulps in air, choking.

Fish says, *"Slowly, Rhyonna."*

Over to the sandy shore Fish swims. Rhyonna floats off with her wings held tight against her sides. Slumping to the water, Rhyonna coughs.

"Thank you! Fish, thank you for saving me!"

"Gladly, my friend! Save happily."

Crying, then laughing, then choking with fear Rhyonna weeps, "I will never fly."

Fish's eyes acknowledge her pain.

"Glow bright. Find Rhyonna. Fly possible."

Rhyonna leans on Fish surveying the beach. "I need to go to the thistles by the gray caves to wait for Keegan, Caddee, and Prince Blaire."

"Rough, danger."

"My Friends and I must defeat Zzuf, the horrid fluff that lives in these caves. Our village, as well as the Ladybugs, ants, you, and all others are in danger."

"Explain, curious. Eat ants."

"Fish." Rhyonna emphasizes, "That horror, gray fluff eats everything."

"Gray fluff?"

Fish wiggles nervously.

"Understand, tell."

"That gray fluff caught me. It captured the Ladybugs, who protect our BlackBerry bushes."

Fish shudders and wheezes.

"Ants crawled into the caves and picked the fluff. Now the colony has the parasite inside."

Dismayed, Fish pulls into the water.

"Eat ants. Think ick! Take to thistles."

Holding her wings tight, Rhyonna wades into the cold deep water, and floats onto Fish's back. With powerful swaying motions, Fish swims along the edge of the lake looking for the caves.

A warm current of air rushes through Rhyonna's hair. The spray falls on her skin as fresh rain. The sun sparkles through the water on Fish's emerald colors, the silver in his scales glisten in ripples of water.

For moments, Rhyonna dismisses her dreadful task. Fish is a wealth of reassurance. Rhyonna wants to stay on him forever. Breaking to the surface of the water, Fish approaches the thistles.

"Prickles scratch. Cause ick."

"Fish, I will wait here for my Friends, who come soon. The sun is hot and the evening will be warm enough to dry my wing. I will hide in the thistles."

Fish slides into the deeper water.

"Tell friends. Explain fluff."

"Thanks, Fish. You are a best friend, forever."

"Look for yours, tell."

19 - THE PLAN

TURNING TO THE HORROR AHEAD, Rhyonna wades to the thistles through the slippery gray water. The floating moss surrounds her and sticks to her dress resembling the dreaded fluff.

Rhyonna's head throbs with pain, a bit from the fall into the water and bit from the Tawnyee Flyers flying alone to the village. Rhyonna is sure they flew back to tell Teacher Caddee. They know by looking at her wings and that dry string mound not to follow and go directly to the village.

Ahead are the caves, sliced by the battle between the wind currents and water ripples. The thistles are the safest place, close to the ant colony. With the ants and her Friends, Rhyonna will defeat the monster.

Climbing onto the clay beach, Rhyonna shouts, "Keegan, Caddee, Prince Blaire, where are you?" Her shout warns of an intruder. A hush greets, the others quiet. Her Friends are not here.

Sitting on the warm mud, Rhyonna gently moves her wings back and forth to dry. The spiders' webbing falls off. Rhyonna laughs! As her wings heal, the light yellow spots do match her yellow dress, which again is muddy. These sours show Rhyonna's adventure, marks of courage, as Mother Emma said.

Zzuf is loathing and clueless. When Zzuf eats everything, it dies. INSANE! That parasite is wicked. Must be the intense hunger of being alone in the cold, wet clays. Growing in the dark makes Zzuf evil.

Miserable memories and mildew odor from the thistles cause regret to surge. The best flyer wanted to do everything. Shivering, Rhyonna assures herself. "I will defeat Zzuf."

Gentle taps awaken Rhyonna from her laments.

"*Faery Rhyonna,*" an ant speaks.

"*Brawny Faery from the Dandelion,*" another ant speaks.

Rhyonna sits up. "I know those taps!"

"*You know us, Scouts Neddy and Rue from the cave time.*"

"My guides who helped me climb out of the caves and talk to Queen Floree."

Rhyonna breathes in her fears, and then pats her Friends.

"We thought you were home," Scout Rue asks.

"I was home. The wind blew me back."

"Don't fret, we are here," says Scout Neddy.

Where are Scouts Bryn and Fay?"

Scout Neddy speaks, *"Most sadness. Bryn and Fay had the horrid fluff in them."*

"That is most sad and tragic."

"They tasted to see if right as food," Scout Rue adds.

"How are Queen Floree and the colony?"

Scout Neddy speaks, *"Our Queen Floree is healthy and busy."*

Over the thistles, Rhyonna sees her Friends flying down the hill. They navigate slowly through the tangle of prickles. Standing, Rhyonna waves and shouts, "I'm here, over here!"

Shouts return, "Rhyonna!"

Suddenly, Keegan picks Rhyonna up and swings her around. Then he hugs and gives his warmest kiss on her lips. Before recovering, Caddee and Prince Blaire offer hugs.

"These are the Scouts, my guides through the ant colony, who saved me."

Caddee reminds Rhyonna, "We know them. The Scouts told us about Zzuf."

"*We met here at the caves,*" adds Scout Neddy.

"*Our Queen will be delighted your Friends come to help,*" says Scout Rue.

Scouts Neddy and Rue extend many approving taps on Rhyonna's Friends.

"*We tell Our Queen Floree,*" says Scout Neddy.

"*Guard Prior will awake you early,*" Scout Rue adds.

"*The entrance is at the top of this hill,*" Scout Neddy directs.

"*When inside, we will escort you to our Queen Floree,*" Scout Rue adds.

"I get queasy when I remember Zzuf." Dizzy, nose snuffled, and eyes burning, Rhyonna sits. "I hate Zzuf, the fluff is HORROR!"

Caddee holds Rhyonna. "You know what Zzuf does."

"Brawny Faery, because of your courage we are here to help," offers Scout Neddy.

"Finally, Zzuf removed from ours and the others," Scout Rue declares.

Keegan takes Rhyonna's hand. "The fluff is gone tomorrow."

Rhyonna soaks in the comfort and support of her Friends. "We rid Zzuf from ours, I am ready!"

Holding Keegan's hand, Rhyonna follows Caddee and Prince Blaire deep into the thickets. With their knives, Keegan and Prince Blaire clear a place to sit.

Caddie gives everyone yellow pollen she brought in her pack. "We expected you were here. Your Fish told his friends to watch for us. My Fish saw us walking along the beach of the lake and told us to go to the thistles by the gray caves."

Keegan reaches for the pollen. "The thistles are a perfect place, good protection."

"Thistle flowers offer a soft bed for sleep during the night." Prince Blaire says as he brushes yellow pollen from his face.

"The Tawnyee Flyers wondered why a thistle for a King," laughs Caddee.

Keegan chuckles, "A beautiful, fun place for a King to relax." The laughter relaxes Rhyonna.

Caddee says, "Healer Leanna sent salve for your wings and spider webbing. She said to go slow and no stressing; healing takes time."

Caddee cleans Rhyonna's wings. "I like the yellow spots."

"The sours show my courage."

"Most notable spots I've seen," comments Prince Blaire.

Keegan jokes, "Everyone will want them."

Frowning first, then Rhyonna laughs. "Not the way I got them."

Caddee finishes the wrapping. "Healer Leanna said only for the night, the webbing comes off tomorrow."

Rhyonna stresses, "I face another trauma."

Prince Blaire comments, "We depend on you."

"I wanted to fly before confronting Zzuf."

"Rhyonna, you are not alone," says Keegan.

"We understand your uncertainties, we have doubts about our skills," Caddee sympathizes. "We work together. Faeries have amazing powers."

"We come to help overpower this horrifying parasite," Prince Blaire offers.

Keegan consoles, "Tomorrow, you will be the risk-taking Rhyonna we admire." Prince Blaire and Caddee agree.

Rhyonna appreciates their hope and knows faeries have amazing powers, not always known. "Yes, I have my Friends, the ants, and the spiders. Able to fly or not, I am capable." As a reassuring spreads, Rhyonna holds the hands of her Friends. Courage, power, and support join their task.

To lighten all nervousness, Rhyonna recalls, "The Tawnyee Flyers were sure surprised when the wind blew the dandelion seeds into the sky, then whisked me up higher."

"They flew into the village, panicked, shouting, 'Rhyonna's gone!'" Caddee adds, "Every villager came. I had a hard time settling the Flyers. Finally Princess Lessie Shelly explained that the wind took the dandelion seeds over the lake and you floated off, shouting, 'Fly to the village. Get help.'"

"The Queen and King asked for Caddee, Keegan, and myself to come forward." Prince Blaire continues, "We were surprised when they asked if we would search for you. Queen Mother said, 'Her Friends know where Rhyonna went, where Zzuf is, and are best to work with the ants.'"

"The villagers cheered when we flew into the Oaks," brags Keegan.

"What about the safety of the Tawnyee Flyers?"

"The King looked at them because they whined to go." Caddee explains, "He said loud and clear, 'Tawnyee Flyers, you are to stay with your parents at all times, in the home flowers. You are not to visit or talk to another Flyer or NO flying lessons with Rhyonna.' Then he looked at their parents."

"The four recognized clearly what the King meant; they now understand consequences," Prince Blaire adds.

"I think the four felt relieved," says Caddee. "They know about the battle with Zzuf."

Rhyonna reminds her Friends, "We need to contact home. I blew away on a seed. Then you left to search for me."

Keegan says, "This time the Queen and King and our parents should know we are in the thistles."

Caddee agrees with Rhyonna, "We do need to channel home to tell everyone Rhyonna is safe."

"Let's do the fire circle. The heat and light from the flames will send a fast message."

Prince Blaire and Keegan gather dry thistle leaves and stems and stack them into a pile. Keegan clacks two rocks together and sparks fly. A spark leaps into the dry thistles and smoke gently flows up into the evening. With her Friends, Rhyonna sits in a circle around the smoke. Flames appear.

"This is perfect," approves Caddee.

"Rhyonna, do you want to go?" asks Keegan.

"Let Prince Blaire go. The Queen wants to know he is okay."

Caddee says, "Keegan and I will chant. Rhyonna, save your strength for tomorrow."

With her Friends, Rhyonna stares into the dancing flames. The dance is the entrance. As the flames reach and crackle, Keegan and Caddee chants, "Prince Blaire home you go! HOME YOU GO!"

With eyes opened wide, Prince Blaire becomes quiet as he concentrates on the flames. After many minutes, Prince Blaire looks up, smiling. "That was good. My parents are happy I appeared. They are pleased Rhyonna is with us. The Queen Mother will tell Rhyonna's parents and the villagers. All hopes are with us."

Keegan looks seriously at Rhyonna. "Tell us specifically what is in the caves!"

Smoke dances as memories chase her stress. Rhyonna searches for the right words to describe something that no one could imagine. Her Friends wait patiently.

"The caves are gray and wet. Water from the lake seeps in and runs along the floors. Fluffed forms lay all over. Odors are hideous death. Spores from Zzuf land on the damp walls and in the puddles of syrup. Thin hairs spread and reach from the walls and the moldy, rotting hornet."

Keegan, Prince Blaire, and Caddee shiver with disgust.

Needing warmth, Rhyonna stirs the fire. "The Grayed Creatures threw me into syrupy, sticky goop. Then I was dragged to a cave with frightened Ladybugs. The horrid fluff devoured them when they ate the moldy, fluffed syrup."

To gather more warmth, Rhyonna stirs the fire again. "My hope was the ants, who made a hole in the clay wall and stole the fluff."

Caddee asks, "What was the ant colony like inside?"

"Eerie, at first, dark and steep, then tranquil and pleasant. There were movements I could not see because my glow dimmed. My four guides, the Scouts, took me to the different chambers for the ants to meet me. Their taps were light and tickled. The ants were happy to meet a faery. Queen Floree was especially kind."

Keegan interrupts, "Did you see the ant's entrance into the caves?"

"Pushed up from below into a dark tunnel, I was too exhausted to notice."

"We need a strategy," states Keegan.

"The Orb Weavers will help us, the ants, and you, my dearest Friends," Rhyonna emphasizes.

"The fluff does dry up in the sun?" asks Prince Blaire.

"In the hot sun!"

"We need to drive Zzuf from the damp cave into the heat outside," suggests Keegan.

"Scout Neddy said they found that garlic and primrose oils kept the fluff from growing on them," offers Caddee.

Keegan adds, "Let's ask Queen Floree if the ants can use the oils on Zzuf."

"The Orb Weavers will spin webs around the opening to keep Zzuf from escaping. The ants can smother Zzuf when outside in the sunlight," states Rhyonna.

Prince Blaire asks, "How will the Orb Weavers know where to weave their webs?"

"Or which cave?" wonders Keegan.

Rhyonna laughs, "Spiders and ants do talk to each other."

"I've never seen an ant in a spider web," notes Prince Blaire.

"A bit of magic will be with us tomorrow," offers Caddee.

Prince Blaire says, "We need magic."

"The battle will be more than magic!" states Keegan.

With nervous laughter, the challenge is set. Rhyonna studies the commitment of her Friends. Uneasiness with no hesitation; they are ready. Rhyonna pushes forth courage and purpose to disguise her thoughts of losing, maybe death.

"We need to rest for power and strength and clear minds," Caddee suggests.

Prince Blaire cuts down dry thistle flowers, places them on the ground, and cuts them up. He then spreads their softness on the ground for beds. With her Friends, Rhyonna snuggles into the night.

After a while, able to conceal her anxieties about the coming battle, Rhyonna in her humble way offers, "Thank you, dearest Friends, for being with me. I value your friendship with my life."

Keegan assures, "We will smash the fluff."

"VICTORY," states Rhyonna to stop her doubts.

All glows dim for their sleep.

The nightmares come for Rhyonna. The odors of the cave drift while spreading spores grab. Rhyonna crawls through dark caves searching for away out, only to fall into slippery fluffed syrup.

20 - THE DESCENT

AS THE SUN FLASHES through the thistles, Guard Prior taps Rhyonna. Opening her eyes, Rhyonna chokes, "Tomorrow is here."

Guard Prior smiles in an ant's proud way. *"Brawny Faery, are you ready?"*

Although nervous about the challenge, Rhyonna smiles at Guard Prior. "I'm glad today came. I'm ready." Slowly, Rhyonna stands with the help of the mighty guard.

"Our Queen Floree said to tell Brawny Rhyonna Faery we owe the life of the colony to her alertness and persistence."

Her Friends awake to Guard's taps. The three giggle. Guard Prior asks, *"Too hard?"*

"No," replies Keegan. "Your taps are so light they tickle."

Rhyonna suggests, "Pat Guard Prior, see if she laughs." Guard Prior laughs in an ant's way.

"Dearest Faeries, are you ready for the battle?"

"Yes, just a bit tense," offers Keegan. Prince Blaire and Caddee nod in agreement.

After the greetings, Caddee unwraps the webbing from Rhyonna's wings. Rhyonna flutters her wings and asks, "Is Queen Floree ready for us to destroy Zzuf and cleanse the horror from the caves?"

"Brave Faeries, Our Queen Floree waits for you."

Although every one is ready to destroy Zuff, fear appears. Rhyonna walks slowly with Guard Prior. Her Friends follow behind walking through the thistles, climbing up the hill, and over pebbles to the entry of the colony.

Coming from the hole are feelers from two smaller ants who climb out and eagerly tap Rhyonna.

"Scout Neddy here, ready for your climb into our colony."

"Scout Rue here, your guides to Our Queen Floree."

Pleased, Guard Prior's feelers wiggle in the air. *"I sent a message before I woke you. Too dark inside the tunnels for me."*

Rhyonna pats Guard Prior. "Will we see you there?"

"I'm to watch this entrance until I'm called."

Prince Blaire looks into the hole. "It goes straight down, a deep tunnel."

Keegan requests, "May we keep our glows on?"

"Keep your lights dim," says Scout Neddy.

"Our colony lives in the safety of darkness," Scout Rue adds.

Caddee sighs, "Straight down."

Prince Blaire complains, "Crawling?"

"Climbing down," corrects Rhyonna. "Hang onto the notches the ants dug in the side of the wall. You will climb down a ladder. Remember to turn your glows very low, almost off. We can still see."

Scout Neddy climbs in first. Next is Rhyonna, who carefully tucks her wings, holds onto the edge, finds the notches, and slips her feet into a step.

Keegan follows. "The dark is alive. My eyes dance colors."

Caddee climbs down. "I like the quiet. My ears sing."

Prince Blaire puts his head into the tunnel. "Is it stuffy down there?"

Rhyonna answers from inside, "The smells are of flowers in the Meadow. Come down feet first."

"Can I breathe?" Prince Blaire asks.

Rhyonna shouts up, "The ants funnel air into the tunnels. You can feel the air move."

Prince Blaire climbs into the tunnel. "I like the sweet smell."

Scout Rue follows as the last.

With her Friends, Rhyonna descends deeper into the ground under the thistles. Many grateful taps touch Rhyonna as well as her Friends.

Prince Blaire asks, "Rhyonna, why are the ants gently tapping on us?"

"The ants feel where they are as they work."

"The taps tickle," giggles Caddee.

"This is serious," cautions Keegan.

"The feelers do tickle," chuckles Prince Blaire.

"The ants also check to make sure we are not intruders."

"Are we safe?" asks Prince Blaire.

"You smell like the ant colony, grass and thistles. You are Faeries." Scout Neddy waits at the first landing.

Caddee asks, "Where did the tunnel go?"

"We are in the brooding chambers near the top of the colony where nurses protect the pupae," informs Rhyonna.

Prince Blaire observes, "The air is fresh and warm."

Captain Keegan inhales, "Buttercups in spring."

"Here come the taps," warns Rhyonna

"Welcome, dearest Faeries." says a kind voice.

With glows dimmed, Rhyonna with her Friends watch the nurses moving the babies.

Caddee observes, "The pupae are transparent. I see babies inside."

Scout Neddy descends along a tunnel tilting down. Rhyonna with her Friends follow.

"We travel to Queen Floree's chamber, which is in the middle of the colony, through the nurseries."

Prince Blaire asks, "Why so many rooms, each with a fragrance?"

"Separate nurseries have the guards, sorters, scouts, gatherers, the nurses, Queens, and a few

Kings. The scents change because the nurses feed the babies different seeds, flowers, or nectars to make the different types of workers."

"Thank you, Brawny Rhyonna Faery. Thank you. You saved us," sing many tiny voices.

Caddee asks, "Why do the baby ants tap and want to kiss us?"

"You mean pressing jaws to our mouths," Keegan adds.

Rhyonna laughs. "Ants share with each ant. Their way of knowing the outside, the time, the weather, what we ate. Everything."

"The children are so happy, so reassured. No wonder the ants work so hard; they are loved in their childhood," Caddee remarks.

"Rhyonna, how do you know so much?" asks Prince Blaire.

"Scouts Neddy and Rue told me."

With her Friends, Rhyonna climbs down another tunnel onto the next floor.

"Be careful, and step lightly," cautions Scout Neddy.

"We enter our Queen Floree's chamber," Scout Rue announces.

Keegan inhales, "Chrysanthemums."

A small ant taps Rhyonna then her Friends. *"Remember, Brawny Faery Rhyonna, I'm mighty Aide Erstwood, our Queen Floree's Messenger."*

Caddee observes, "You are tiny, not large like Guard Prior on the hill."

"Yes! I am quick, hide easily, and attack fast. I investigated the caves. Bad things grow down there. Hornets and Ladybugs melted into fluffy piles."

"Rhyonna lived in that and survived," admires Prince Blaire.

"Brawny Rhyonna is one strong Faery. Zzuf has few helpers. The ants are healthy, thanks to Brawny Rhyonna."

Aide Erstwood leads Rhyonna with her Friends into a large flat chamber, which glows orange. Keegan, Caddee, and Prince Blaire "awe!" seeing the Queen. Before Rhyonna can distinguish who is in the chamber, Aide Erstwood requests, *"Faeries, please, turn off your glows."*

Then Aide Erstwood announces, *"Our Queen Floree. Brawny Rhyonna Faery is here with her Friends."*

Queen Floree shuffles with a bustle of sounds and fragrance. *"Welcome my Brawny Rhyonna. You are well?"*

Rhyonna curtseys, "Your Majesty, yes! Happily my wings heal."

Very gently, Queen Floree taps Rhyonna's wings. Sighs of relief come from the Queen. *"You will fly!"*

"Your Majesty, Queen Floree, these are my Friends: Captain Keegan of the Junior Patrol, Teacher Caddee to the Wee Ones, and Prince Blaire, Someday-to-be-our-King."

Queen Floree tenderly taps each. *"Welcome to the Ant Colony in the Thistles on the Hill near the Lake. Welcome 'Someday-to-be-King.' We become allies."*

Prince Blaire curtseys, "Yes, Your Majesty, Queen Floree. Our village is ready."

Keegan curtseys and asks, "Your Majesty, Queen Floree, please, might I brighten my glow?"

"Yes, Captain Keegan, light must help you understand."

Orange glow fills the room, revealing the Queen as a huge golden mass while nurses busily clean, rub oils, and feed the Queen. "Why so quiet?"

Rhyonna politely says, "Your Majesty, Queen Floree, you are huge!"

The Queen squirms, and from behind her, a nurse carries a light, clear sack. The nurse passes by, carrying the egg in her mouth and front legs. "That is my egg, ready for care."

"Yes," acknowledges Rhyonna. "Your Majesty, how did your children get well?"

"We were greatly distressed, when we heard your words about Zzuf. We finally realized why workers disappeared, especially the ones who ate the fluff. The ants tending the garlic and primrose had no fluff on them."

"Garlic and primrose oil are the potions the Healer rubs on my sours."

"Yes! We had the same answer. We ate and rubbed the garlic and primrose oils on us."

"I'm so pleased your ant colony is safe."

"Guard Prior says you are ready to smother the parasite."

"Your Majesty, we will enter caves of Zzuf and drive it out a tunnel into the thistle patch."

Keegan adds, "The spiders said they would help with webs."

"The spiders weave their webs. Spider Erwina brings confidence to our task."

Nurses enter, carrying garlic and primrose creams. Aide Erstwood taps Rhyonna, *"Rub the creams on your skin for protection."*

"We also want you to eat raw garlic and drink primrose oil for protection against breathing in spores."

While drinking the primrose oil and eating the raw garlic, Keegan, Prince Blaire, and Caddee gag and choke. Rhyonna chuckles "Now you know what these tastes are. Cherry bark is the best."

Aide Erstwood agrees, *"Chewing cherry bark is a tremendous help. I will call for the bitter."*

"Your Majesty, when Zzuf is outside, can the ants spray Zzuf with garlic and primrose oils to stop the spores from spreading?"

"Yes, Bravest Faeries, We have the oils. We will spray everything. Zzuf! Clay! Dirt! Plants! You! Us!"

Captain Keegan asks, "Your Majesty, might we have sticks to help us?"

"We have thought of this already."

Ants carry in large thistle thorns and pass these sticks to Rhyonna then her Friends.

"Guard Prior sends the fighting sticks for your battle," Scout Neddy informs.

"The Guard wishes you well and is ready," extends Scout Rue.

"Your Majesty, can your ants follow us into the caves when we push Zzuf outside to spray the mold growing inside?"

Queen Floree lifts her large feelers in approval. *"Yes, my Brawny Rhyonna. We have sprayed some of the caves already. We plan to seal the caves with mud to seal them forever."*

Queen Floree taps approval on Rhyonna, then her Friends. *"Thank you, Bravest Faeries from BlackBerry Village. Finally, death for the horrid, cruel Zzuf."*

Rhyonna curtseys. "Your Majesty, Queen Floree, you are a great caring mother." Then hugs and clings to the Queen as if never to meet.

"We sense fear and hesitation from the Brawny Rhyonna. Where is the braveness that talked to us about this horror?"

"Your Majesty, I lack bravery because my frolic caused harm to my wings."

To Rhyonna, Queen Floree gives a consoling embrace. *"Brawny Rhyonna, you found a parasite ready to eat all of us. Together WE end this horror."*

As her Friends curtsey to Queen Floree, Rhyonna studies them. Keegan stands close to her, protecting; he is Captain and self-assured and handles obstacles with cunning, a decisive challenger. Prince Blaire is here because of his friendship with Keegan, a devoted friend. He is nervous and fidgets, however will defend when challenged. Friend Caddee is here because of their friendship, closest of friends, always together. Caddee is smart and steady.

Rhyonna curtseys to Queen Floree. "Your Majesty. We are READY!"

Aide Erstwood directs, *"Scouts Neddy and Rue will lead with their feelers. Their touches will tell which way to move. We have battled huge monsters and won."*

As Scouts Neddy and Rue pat and hug their Queen Floree, Rhyonna hears slight whimpers.

Aide Erstwood advises, *"Remember to use your thistle sticks. Move slowly. Keep alert. Turn off your glows. I follow behind to direct the cleanup."*

Walking down the tunnel with Scouts Neddy and Rue, Rhyonna with the greatest alertness and caution is with her strong, determined fighting team: Captain Keegan, Prince Blaire, and Caddee. Along with the ants and spiders, her Friends will make a significant attack. Rhyonna will do her best beyond her best to defeat horrid Zzuf.

21 - THE BATTLE

DROPPING INTO A STEEP TUNNEL, which goes straight down, Rhyonna with her Friend follow Scouts Neddy and Rue. Finding a notch in the wall is a task. Climbing seems forever, slow and tedious. Rhyonna intently focuses on the attack. Finally, a hole leads into the grimy, dingy, wet caves. With Keegan's help, protecting her wings, Rhyonna carefully drops through the hole.

Stillness rings through the caves. The clammy, cold air stands stagnant, filled with bitter sour. With glows dimmed, noses held, and sticks positioned, Rhyonna's fighting team carefully advances. Remembering the horror, Rhyonna stops. Keegan gently pushes her forward.

Prince Blaire observes, "Mounds have the fluff growing from them."

"Once hornets and Ladybugs," chokes Rhyonna, remembering frightful whimpers.

Caddee gags, "How awful, slime everywhere."

"The bizarre parasite lives down here," Scout Neddy affirms.

"Why does light shine in here?" asks Keegan.

"We are by an entrance," informs Scout Neddy.

"Zzuf lives in the caves under the thistle bank," Scout Rue explains.

"Gray fluff is all over everything," coughs Caddee as she steps over a pile.

"Do not get any on you," warns Rhyonna.

"Here's a toadstool," remarks Prince Blaire.

"I ate those," replies Rhyonna, shaking.

Scout Neddy rises up. Her legs and feelers move fast. With her Friends, Rhyonna turns. A dark horror creeps along the cave behind them. Gray clouds swell with souring mildew and engulf the air.

Keegan whispers, "Zzuf is behind us."

Zzuf bellows in a hollow, empty voice,

"See Faeries!

"Sweet Faeries!

"Rhyonna me."

The fighting team moves towards the entrance.

With angry boldness, Rhyonna turns and stands in front of Zzuf. "Yes, I brought Faeries, ants, and spiders to destroy you, horrid fluff."

Scout Neddy whispers to the team, *"Slip into the cave on your left."*

In an instant, Rhyonna joins her Friends. Zzuf passes them and drags itself to the cave opening.

"We are behind Zzuf. Walk silently," says Scout Neddy.

Zzuf stands in the light at the entrance, looking, almost waiting.

"It's nothing but long fluffy hair reaching," gags Caddee.

"Dangerous fluff," warns Rhyonna. "Notice Zzuf carries the hornet's stinger."

Keegan whispers, "Shhhh, quiet."

Scout Rue warns, *"Zzuf heard you, it turns."*

"Attack!" shouts Keegan. "AaGGgghh!"

First Keegan and Prince Blaire heave toward Zzuf, then Scouts Neddy and Rue. Rhyonna and Caddee follow. Zzuf staggers backward toward the opening. Prince Blaire and Keegan drive their sticks at Zzuf, who stumbles. They poke again and again.

Zzuf lurches at them, then sways backward, closer to the entrance, stopping to spit. Spores cloud the light coming into the cave.

With aggression, Rhyonna thrusts her stick at Zzuf, pushing the fluff into the opening.

Keegan yells, "Push Zzuf out."

Prince Blaire and Scout Neddy edge on the right. Caddee and Scout Rue flank on the left. Rhyonna and Keegan attack from the middle. Zzuf reels into the light, exposing a blurred maze of fluff on a wasted hornet shell.

"The light blinds Zzuf. LUNGE!" Keegan shouts.

Zzuf spits more spores and stumbles as if falling.

"Looks like Zzuf dies," Caddee yells, relaxing her stance.

"Zzuf fools," Scout Neddy shouts.

Again Keegan and Prince Blaire lunge at the fluff. Zzuf tumbles into the light. Scout Neddy and Rue jump on Zzuf, who twists from their jaws. Swelling, Zzuf causes its hairs to reach out, hundreds of tiny long hairs glow, transparent.

"Push Zzuf farther out!" Guard Prior yells.

In full force, Rhyonna swipes her stick at Zzuf, who backs into the glaring sun.

Up Keegan, Caddee, and Prince Blaire fly and poke their sticks at Zzuf. Rhyonna, in agonizing memory and nausea, stabs again and again at Zzuf. Instantly, Rhyonna flies up, her wings beating as fast as her stabs. "You disgusting horror, you ball of fluff. You parasite, you're gone!"

Rhyonna moves Zzuf out the entrance. Webs from the Orb Weavers entangle the thistles, building a cage around the edges and over the top of the cave entry.

Backing farther into the webbed space, Zzuf thrusts its stinger at Rhyonna.

"Get its stinger!" yells Keegan.

Flying, Rhyonna grabs the stinger. Her Friends lunge brutally at the fluff with their sticks. Zzuf, losing balance, falls. Rasping, expanding, Zzuf swells larger and larger.

A foul blowing of rotting death slides through the air.

"KERRCHOO!" rumbles Zzuf!

Fluff and spores explode into the air.

Zzuf disappears into gray floating strings swirling around. The hot sun strikes millions of hairy filaments. Stunned, Rhyonna, her Friends, the ants, spiders, and all the others watching, stop motionless without sound, dazed.

Finally Guard Prior shouts, *"SPRAY!"*

Oils fly into the air, reflecting light as fine dew, and sticking to the long hairs and spores of Zzuf. This glop lands and sticks on Rhyonna, Keegan, Prince Blaire, Caddee, Guard Prior, Scouts Neddy and Rue, Spider Erwina, every spider, and every ant. Rhyonna and her Friends stand soaked with oils and the dissolving fluff.

This glop sticks to the thistles, pebbles, spider webs, everywhere, and on everything. The oily tangled fluff resembles morning dew in an awaking day. Astonished, Rhyonna witnesses with all the others, the hideous spores drown in the oils and disappear in the heat of the sun.

More ants rush through the webbing and again spray the garlic and primrose oils. Then more ants run down the hill from everywhere, spraying everything again.

Rhyonna holds her nose. "Guard Prior, I have never smelled such odor, and that smell is not coming from the fluff."

Her Friends choke, "A dreadful smell."

Guard Prior smiles as an ant does. *"Oh, our famous battle odor."*

"We scent to alert every ant of danger," Scout Neddy informs.

"The odor also warns off predators," adds Scout Rue.

Prince Blaire shakes his head. "That smell I will never forget."

Laughing, Keegan and Caddee agree.

Rhyonna watches the ants busily turn over every rock and all dried leaves and smear them with more garlic and primrose oil. The ground becomes muddied oil; with no traces of Zzuf. The parasitic horror smothered, dead.

Guard Prior points to the cave. *"Now we seal all openings with mud."*

Rhyonna turns toward the lake and observes a line of ants stretching up to the caves. From ant to ant, they hand mud from one to the next, up the hill to the cave openings. "Let's help."

With Keegan, Prince Blaire, and Caddee, Rhyonna smooths mud into an entrance. Ants pass rocks and press into the mud, while spiders weave their silk into the mud to secure and make closures sturdy. After several hours, all the openings are sealed.

An ant walks up to Scout Neddy. They tap. Scout Neddy turns to Rhyonna. *"We have sprayed the caves with oils."*

Keegan admires, "Ants are fast."

Scout Rue adds, *"Our Queen Floree did not want these horrid spores attacking the vulnerable, innocent others or spreading again into our colony."*

Rhyonna stands, looks around, opens her wings, and raises her arms, shouting, "Everyone, thank you all for your support and help. Zzuf, the horrid parasitic fluff, dead, gone from our realms!"

Keegan, Caddee, and Prince Blaire clap and yell their approval. The ants, spiders, and all of the others cheer in their ways. The hurrahs are loud, fulfilling and most gratify for all; realms are safe.

Rhyonna shouts, "I have courageous friends."

Rhyonna notes the ants and spiders smile at her as if they know a secret. Dirt and goop is all over her. Keegan actually looks at the Scouts Neddy and Rue and at Guard Prior to hush them. Prince Blaire and Caddee giggle. Rhyonna says, "We need to wash off the mud and oils at the lake."

22 - RHYONNA'S FLIGHT

WALKING TO THE LAKE for a drink of clean water and to wash, Rhyonna turns to the giant Spider Erwina. "How did the Orb Weavers know today was the day?"

Spider Erwina chuckles in a spider's way. *"Hummingbird Hue, while eating gnats above the lake, saw the four Flyers panic in the air and fly towards the village. On a seed, Brawny Faery Rhyonna hung whimpering, 'Tell my Friends to meet me in the thistles by the caves.' Hue flew directly to Evan Roy, who told Darren Gale, who told me, Spider Erwina. I told the Orb Weavers. We knew exactly where to find the ants, they welcomed our help and knew where Zzuf was. We started weaving our web trap."*

Rhyonna sighs, "Hummingbird Hue heard me?"

Prince Blaire confirms, "Magic in the air."

"The others send their messages faster than Faeries," chuckles Spider Erwina.

Rhyonna pats Spider Erwina. "I have boundless gratitude to the others, and the ways you speak in your realms."

Then Guard Prior stands beside Rhyonna carrying special bundles. *"These come from Aide Erstwood. Our Queen Floree wants your villagers to prosper. These will bring fortune to the Faeries of BlackBerry Village."*

Rhyonna unwraps the first leaf bundle. "Blackberry seeds? How did Queen Floree know?"

"Scouts Neddy and Rue told our Queen Floree."

Scout Neddy confirms, *"Yes, we heard on a Scouting trip. Your villagers were upset because the bushes died. Much worse, the seeds molded."*

Scout Rue adds, *"That includes us and our aphids. No bushes, no honey dew for us."*

Guard Prior respectfully taps Rhyonna. *"Our Queen Floree wants your villagers to know we will not set our aphids on the BlackBerry bushes of the Faeries."*

Scout Rue supports, *"Our Queen Floree wants our colony cleared of misunderstandings."*

Guard Prior hands the second bundle to Rhyonna. Upon opening this package and

A FAERY'S CHALLENGE TO SAVE HER REALM

examining the leaves, Rhyonna sobs both grief and joy. Finally, with much appreciation Rhyonna asks, "How did the ants find the Ladybug eggs?"

Guard Prior states proudly, *"Our Special Scouts Neddy and Rue traveled to the colony across the lake to the mother colony of our Queen Floree."*

Scout Neddy adds, *"Our cousins' territory was not yet harmed by the horror fluff."*

Scout Rue adds, *"They found the eggs and we carefully carry the eggs to you."*

"Prince Blaire will give Queen Tanya and King Grady the packages and the messages. Our villagers will be pleased and will forgive the Ant Colony in the Thistles by the Lake. Queen Floree and her ants will remain our friends."

Prince Blaire promises, "The Faeries will also help the ants. Rhyonna, Keegan, Caddee, and myself will bring syrup in the cold seasons to the colony. Tell Queen Floree these offerings bridge the trust between us, becoming best of allies. The Orb Weavers are our witnesses."

Guard Prior turns to Spider Erwina. *"Our Queen Floree thanks all the Orb Weavers."*

Spider Erwina strokes the large Guard. *"My friends are pleased to save ours and help the others."*

Rhyonna throws her arms around Guard Prior's large head, kissing her, then kisses Scouts Neddy and Rue. The three ants raise their front legs and wiggle their feelers. All the ants follow.

Rhyonna dances around and through the ants giving each taps of happy respect. Her Friends follow. The Orb Weavers and ants also dance in their ways.

After the long dance, Rhyonna curtseys to Guard Prior, Scout Neddy, and Scout Rue.

Guard Prior turns to Rhyonna, *"We knew Brawny Rhyonna Faery would fly."*

The faces of the ants and spiders beam happiness at Rhyonna, who fills with surprise.

"What? FLY?"

With pleased faces Keegan, Prince Blaire, and Caddee smile at Rhyonna.

Keegan asks, "Rhyonna, you know you flew?"

Rhyonna unsure, answers, "NO!"

"Rhyonna, you flew!" assures Caddee.

"Yes!" confirms Prince Blaire.

Rhyonna gasps, "You all saw me fly?"

"When you stabbed Zzuf," says Keegan.

"And grabbed the stinger," Prince Blaire adds.

Rhyonna leaps up. "YES, I remember, when I thought Zzuf had me. I jumped and caught the stinger." Rhyonna dances and sings, "YES" around her Friends, "YES" around the ants, "YES!" around the spiders. Then Rhyonna yells. "I CAN FLY!"

"That's why Guard Prior, Erwina, and Scouts Neddy and Rue smile at me, they saw."

All the others glimmer in Rhyonna's delight and sing, "Rhyonna flies!" Voices echo telling all others in the Oak forests, in the lake, and into the Flowers of the Meadow. All hum the joy for the Brawny Rhyonna Faery, the bravest Flyer of all.

With all her power and strength, Rhyonna jumps, only tumbles. Up flies Keegan and catches Rhyonna in his arms.

Immediately, all the old terror, fears, and concerns of horrid Zzuf rush through Rhyonna. In grief Rhyonna sinks into Keegan's arms sobbing, "I can't fly." Her lost joy falls from the trees and settles with sadness around the others who watch.

Caddee sits on the ground beside Rhyonna. "You're exhausted."

Keegan holds Rhyonna. "This is battle stress. We are all tired."

"You removed an ugly, aggressive horror. This takes energy," compliments Prince Blaire.

Guard Prior, Scouts Neddy and Rue, Spider Erwina, and the others agree.

After a long while Rhyonna admits, "I am tired."

Keegan adds, "You succeeded. You completed a dangerous, incredible task."

"The horror is gone."

The others, who watch and listen, cheer. Through the thistles, over the lake, and into the Meadow their echoes sing. Joy returns to Rhyonna and the others sing her happiness.

Rhyonna laughing, at the same time tears flow, shouts, **"I did fly!"**

"Rhyonna, tomorrow you fly again," Guard Prior says.

"Go slow, you have time," Spider Erwina encourages.

"We sprayed a lot of oil on you," Scout Neddy says.

"Oil is heavy and sticky," Scout Rue adds.

Rhyonna smiles at her Friends. "Yes, I have tomorrow."

Spider Erwina laments, *"The Orb Weavers must tend our webs. We will see you in the Meadow."*

Scouts Neddy and Rue sigh, *"We must go."*

Guard Prior says, *"Remembers us to the wee faeries."*

With her Friends, Rhyonna sits on the clay beach looking out over the lake. The battle was incredible. Fatigued from the ordeal, Rhyonna can hardly move, so walking to the village is no option.

"Majestic. He has room on his back for four Faeries. Hold hands," directs Rhyonna. "Look into the water, and concentrate on Majestic. When you see a Dragonfly's reflection call, 'Majestic.'"

Rhyonna stares into the water and sings, "Come get us, mighty giant of the sky. We need your help."

Caddee chants, "Majestic, Majestic, Majestic."

On their legs, Captain Keegan and Prince Blaire slap, "MA-jest-ic, MA-jest-ic, MA-jest-ic, MA-MA-MA, MA-jest-ic."

In seconds, a mighty gold-green Dragonfly flies to the beach and lands on a rock.

Rhyonna hugs Majestic. "I flew!"

Majestic smiles in a Dragonfly way, *"I know, Faery Rhyonna, who loves to fly. I heard, by way of the ants. All others are proud."*

"Only we are too exhausted to fly home after defeating the horrid Zzuf," sighs Rhyonna.

"I will take you and your Friends."

Majestic walks to Rhyonna. Keegan climbs on first and helps Rhyonna. Caddee climbs up, then Prince Blaire. The Dragonfly's wings reach for the sky. Majestic jumps with a strong push. With open wings pulling down, the air pops. Then he flies with wings whizzing.

Her Friends and Rhyonna are safe; a powerful, confident giant flies over the Oak trees and into the flicker of the shadows to the BlackBerry Village.

23 - THE GIFTS

AS MAJESTIC LANDS on the beach of the creek, Rhyonna sees the Tawnyee Flyers peer from under the BlackBerry bushes. They fly toward her, singing, "Majestic! Rhyonna! Rhyonna is back."

The adults flutter from the BlackBerry bushes, clapping and shouting, "Hurrah!" as they fly to Majestic. The songs of the others pause, so they may listen.

Rhyonna is the first to slide off Majestic. Roars of gratitude burst from the villagers. Their thankfulness melts Rhyonna. For their approval, Rhyonna curtseys.

The villagers retain their jubilance as her Friends Captain Keegan, Teacher Caddee, and Prince Blaire slide from Majestic. The Tawnyee Flyers with all the Wee Ones circle and glide around and around Rhyonna, making her sway. Captain Keegan offers his arm to steady her.

Rhyonna holds up a leaf bundle tied with dried grass for all to see, then hands the bundle to Prince

Blaire, who immediately gives the bundle back to Rhyonna. Back and forth, they hand the bundle, until Rhyonna stops and tenderly grabs Prince Blaire's shoulder and turns him to face the villagers. Prince Blaire hesitates.

Loud enough for all to hear, Rhyonna says, "Prince Blaire has something to share."

Forcefully Rhyonna whispers, "Prince Blaire, this is your right. Someday you will be our King."

Prince Blaire steps forward, "Villagers, you must know, Rhyonna flew as she challenged the horrid parasitic fluff known as Zzuf."

Joy rips through the crowd. Wee Flyers soar and circle her success in the air. After the excitement for Rhyonna's triumph, Prince Blaire continues.

"You must know. Zuff was caught in the webs built by the Orb Weavers. The horrid fluff and spores vanished. DESTROYED! Suffocated with oils of garlic and primrose sprayed on it by the ants. The OTHERS helped Rhyonna as promised."

Admiration flashes, loud shouts burst from the villagers. Wee Flyers somersault in the ringing praise. Prince Blaire will make a strong King.

"Queen Floree of the Ant Colony in the Thistle by the Lake wants the name of the ants cleared of their wrongs to our village. The ants are to be allies!"

The villagers become sullen. The others stop moving, listening.

To the King and Queen, Prince Blaire hands the leaf bundle. He announces, "This is Queen Floree's promise. She gives this bundle to the BlackBerry Tenders as hope for our village success."

Queen Tanya opens the package and holds up, "BlackBerry seeds!"

King Grady asks, "How did this come about?"

"Scout Neddy of the ants told Queen Floree that the villagers worried about food supplies because their BlackBerry bushes died."

Distrust descends from the villagers as they hiss and flutter wings.

"Queen Floree sends the seeds because we stopped a horrid parasite from spreading into the realm of the others. The Queen states her ants will not use our BlackBerry bushes for their aphids."

Rhyonna senses pride for the young Prince, who offers accord with fierce competitors for BlackBerry sugars.

"Our village will give the ant colony syrup in the cold seasons. These offerings will bridge the friendship between us, the Faeries of BlackBerry Village and the Ant Colony in the Thistles by the Lake."

The villagers gleam praise, shouting, "Friendship! Allies for BlackBerry Village!"

Queen Tanya adds, "We transfer the seeds to Rhyonna's family, the Tenders of the BlackBerry bushes." Mother Emma and Father Adair fly forward and hug Rhyonna. Her parents bow to the King and Queen. Rhyonna's Father hugs the package and holds it up.

As the villagers congratulate and hug her parents, Rhyonna holds up another package. This stops the villagers. They calm and become speechless, another gift!

"This gift is from Guard Prior and the Scouts Neddy and Rue, who helped Rhyonna out of the caves."

Queen Tanya and King Grady open the package. They hold green leaves up for all to see. The villagers closely observe, recognizing, eggs. Shouts spring up. "LADYBUGS!" This word echoes among all the others watching, listening.

Queen Tanya announces, "These eggs go to the Tenders of the Ladybugs for hatching." The Tenders fly forward to receive the precious package.

Before any villager sings approve, King Grady announces. "We celebrate Brawny Rhyonna Faery, Flying Teacher for the Wee Flyers. We owe her our lives. Rhyonna is brave beyond what we all know. Because of Rhyonna, our village and our BlackBerry bushes grow safe."

The villagers clap and shake their wings, throwing earned praise to the risk taker, who now values life beyond hers. Facing the villagers, Rhyonna turns and opens her yellowed wings to reveal her brown spots, her courage. More shouts of praise vibrate around Rhyonna for her daring boldness.

King Grady continues, "Keegan, Captain of the Junior Patrol, we salute you; we honor your bravery. My son, Prince Blaire, we honor your concerns for our village. Teacher Caddee, we admire your persistent helpfulness and loyalty to your Friends."

Prince Blaire says to the villagers, "Thank you for appreciating and trusting us with your lives."

Everyone dashes into the air, greeting victory. Rhyonna and her Friends are hugged and hugged.

As the colors of evening appear, Healer Leanna and Mother Emma rescue Rhyonna and walk her to the edge of the BlackBerry bushes. Exhaustion hits and Rhyonna shakes. Mother Emma cuddles Rhyonna and strokes her cold hands and arms.

Healer Leanna asks, "So, dearest Rhyonna, how do your wings feel?"

"I have no clue, just normal. I was so determined; Guard Prior told me I flew when I stabbed Zzuf."

"That's the best way, determination. Flight appearing when in need."

Carefully looking and touching Rhyonna's wings, Healer Leanna admires, "You're covered with oil and bits of mud. Surprisingly, you did fly."

Rhyonna inspects her yellow dress, legs and arms. "I am dirty. The mud and oil came later, the protection the ants sprayed on us. At the lake, we rubbed fresh clay and water over ourselves. I guess the clay got on my wings. Have I hurt them?"

"The tiny holes are gone. Healed! Let me clean your wings one last time."

The warm tincture of jasmine and lavender lulls Rhyonna to sleep. Mother Emma awakes Rhyonna; they walk back to the celebration. Rhyonna sits with her Friends at the King and Queen's table.

The pipers, drummers, and fiddlers appear and the merriment begins.

Tables of carved wood stretch under the BlackBerry bushes. Plates, bowls, cups, knives, and spoons made from stone, wood, and clay lie on top of the tables for everyone's use. The villagers in their best dress bring their finest recipes of delicious treasures: pollens and nectars of all sorts, dried and fresh berries, honeys, fresh and dried seeds from the rye, wheat, oat, and barley fixed in many tasty ways, all kinds of nuts, the beloved Oak acorn mash, and of course, the secret brews made from BlackBerry juice.

Rhyonna answers many questions as villagers hug her again and again. The Tawnyee Flyers flitter around and around her, excited, thrilled for Rhyonna, their Flying Teacher.

While the Villagers sing and dance, Rhyonna slips away with Keegan, and they amble to Dandelion. Keegan helps Rhyonna climb up onto the most fragrant flower. He leans on the edge and stares delicately into Rhyonna's green eyes. "Rhyonna, my best friend, I love you. You have courage beyond all I know. I admire you greatly."

Rhyonna stares into Keegan's blue eyes. "Keegan, my best of friends, I love you."

Until the cooling evening air reminds Dandelion to close, Keegan holds Rhyonna's hand. Then Keegan flies to his flower, his daisy in the meadow. Flying Teacher Rhyonna snuggles inside her Dandelion until sleep overcomes her.

Brawny Rhyonna flitters through the grasses:

Floating,

Gliding,

Soaring,

Spiraling,

With the wind,

Flowing,

Pivoting,

Hanging in the air,

Hovering,

Darting,

Then swoops among the flowers with giant Majestic.

In the morning after the sun awakes Dandelion, Rhyonna stands, flutters her wings, and flies to her favorite rock in the Meadow of Flowers. Warming in the sun, Lender the Lizard moves closer to Rhyonna and then silently sings. Rhyonna joins him, singing her appreciation and gratitude to all others among the flowers in and around the Meadow.

###

CONNECTING . . .

I am pleased you read the story!

Please, send drawings of Rhyonna and her Friends
or questions concerning the Faeries and
the Others of the Realms to
BobbieTales@gmail.com.

To post a review
about Rhyonna's Fright go to
Bobbie Amazon Page.

For stories about Rhyonna and her friends go to
www.BobbieKinkead.com.

Befriend me on Facebook:
Facebook Page BobbieTales - Storytelling,
Facebook Page BobbieTales - ART.
Follow me on Twitter@BobbieTales.
Read my blog, The STORY Realm.

STORIES TO COME

The Elfin Letters Series

Book 1 - As It Happened, the Village

I knew there was trouble when I set my eyes on wee darling Lassie JooJee. She made a trap and put kaJ's favorite jellybeans inside. We watched from the tree. I saw kaJ's face; he wanted these beans. He smacked his lips together.

"Now, kaJ, know this …" He cut me off.

"Ole Elf, that girl child can never catch me."

"kaJ, she's a young child, they have magic, no limits. Stay away from the candy beans, which is a foolish leprechaun trap. WE are ELVES. Do I need to tie you to the tree for the Sheeghashee to guard?"

kaJ snubbed me. He would learn soon enough about the magic of the human realm.

That's how these Elfin Letters started.

Book 2 - As It Became, the Shopkeepers

Aunt Millie interviews the elves, trolls, and faeries for her "Book of Families." When the book comes up missing, Aunt Millie's desperate search begins, because she wrote more than enough gossip on each villager and spirit in the gardens.

Excerpt from a letter to the human Lassies:

Dearest Lassies, Queen Kyra Faye Here:

We Elves have a Birth Granting party. When I announce the twin's names they will receive gifts, wishes for health, love, or prosperity. The wishes We fear are the vague ones like, "May they take a long trip!" I must ask the grantor, "Where? How? When?" If the grantor says, "When the time comes." This means the granter plants control, which is a trick: pleasant or entangled. Fairies, Trolls, and Elves all go through the Birth Granting, which is why we are or should be respectful to each other.

Book 3 - As It Is Now, Magick

Excerpt from a letter to the human Lassies:

Dearest Lassies, Queen Kyra Fae Here:

Know, Lassies, you may not visit us. You must know the tale of the earlier centuries when people told untrue lies about us. So, whenever seen by humans, a blinding spell was put on their eyes, to see no longer the others of the spirited folk.

Because you provide us with Rainbow Village in the OakGrove Gardens, giving us homes and including the wonderful treats, gifts, and letters; WE, elves and faeries of the SECRET CIRCLE show our respect and honor you as part of our MAGIC.

To enter, come of calm heart, go to the dancing ground inside the camellia trees, and draw a large circle. Sprinkle sugar and colored candies here and there inside the circle to cook. Light your candles and sit in your directions. WE will be around the circle, singing and dancing. Listen for us.

WE begin!

ABOUT THE AUTHOR

Bobbie Kinkead is a creative illustrator, animated storyteller, and empowering writer. As a child, drawing and painting were her ways of depicting stories. After schooling in the arts, Bobbie Kinkead is an accomplished writer as well as a superb storyteller. Today, with these tools, she blends her skills of illustrating with written and spoken words to produce stories for others to enjoy.